"It's a girl?"

"Yes," the doctor said. "I think you're farther along than eight months. I think she's about to come two weeks early. She might even be six pounds."

"Is that good?"

"That means you can take her home after a couple of days."

Lucy closed her eyes and tears rolled down her cheeks. John knew the problem immediately. He put his arms around her and brought her face to his chest, turning her into him. "It's all right, Lucy. You can come home with me. We'll give your baby a home."

She just shook her head. "I can't stay, John. He'll find me," she said between sobs. "I need to go away!" Lucy sniffed and then gasped as another pain hit her.

John held her tighter. "Honey, we'll talk about that later. Right now you're going to have a baby."

Dear Reader,

Most of you don't need an introduction to the Randalls, but there could be someone out there who picks up this book without knowing anything about this magical family living in Rawhide, Wyoming. When the Randalls first appeared in 1995, I couldn't have imagined they would become such a big part of my life. Over the years, the family has grown in many ways, and they have provided me with many different types of stories.

I don't try to write message books, but that's how John Randall's story turned out. Violence in any form is abhorrent, and I can't stand to think that horrible things happen to people every day. If you are in a situation like Lucy's, I hope you escape and maybe find your own version of a Randall, a hero who'll share life's adversities and celebrate the good things with you.

We're counting down now—there are only three more unattached Randalls. Drew, Josh and Casey are awaiting their stories. Then we'll have to end this series, because I don't want to write the deaths of Red and Mildred. So prepare yourself. People have suggested I do a prequel of the Randalls, but I don't do historicals. I'll try to come up with other stories that you'll like as much as these ones and we'll start another journey as exciting and adventurous as the Randalls of Rawhide, Wyoming.

I hope you enjoy John's story. Happy reading!

Judy Christenberry

Judy Christenberry
A RANDALL HERO

Special Treat!

HARLEQUIN®

TORONTO • NEW YORK • LONDON
AMSTERDAM • PARIS • SYDNEY • HAMBURG
STOCKHOLM • ATHENS • TOKYO • MILAN • MADRID
PRAGUE • WARSAW • BUDAPEST • AUCKLAND

ISBN-13: 978-0-373-75197-6
ISBN-10:   0-373-75197-4

A RANDALL HERO

Copyright © 2008 by Judy Christenberry.

www.eHarlequin.com

Printed in U.S.A.

ABOUT THE AUTHOR

Judy Christenberry has been writing romances for over fifteen years because she loves happy endings as much as her readers do. A former French teacher, Judy now devotes herself to writing full-time. She hopes readers have as much fun with her stories as she does. She spends her spare time reading, watching her favorite sports teams and keeping track of her two daughters. Judy lives in Texas. You can find out more about Judy and her books at www.judychristenberry.com.

Books by Judy Christenberry

HARLEQUIN AMERICAN ROMANCE

*Brides for Brothers
†Tots for Texans
**Children of Texas
‡Dallas Duets

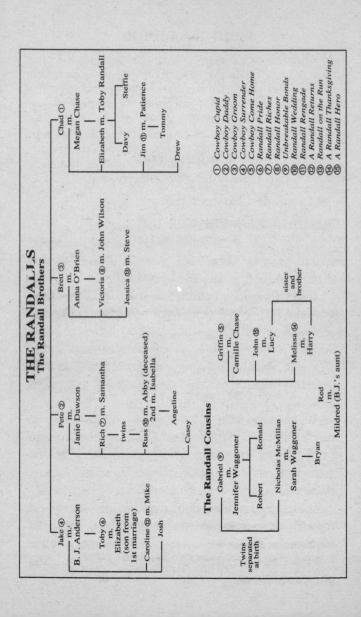

THE RANDALLS
The Randall Brothers

① Cowboy Cupid
② Cowboy Daddy
③ Cowboy Groom
④ Cowboy Surrender
⑤ Cowboy Come Home
⑥ Randall Pride
⑦ Randall Riches
⑧ Randall Honor
⑨ Unbreakable Bonds
⑩ Randall Wedding
⑪ Randall Renegade
⑫ A Randall Returns
⑬ Randall on the Run
⑭ A Randall Thanksgiving
⑮ A Randall Hero

Chapter One

John Randall regretted the past few hours.

A trip to see an old college buddy appear in a rodeo had turned into a marathon when his friend lassoed him into a steak dinner and a few beers.

Every time John had tried to leave, his friend announced he had one more story to tell their companions about their college escapades.

Now he was finally on the road home—two hours late and a hundred miles from home. And the last seventy of them were on the two-lane road that led to Rawhide.

When he left the main road, he settled in for a relaxed drive. At ten o'clock he didn't expect to run into much traffic. But about ten miles down the road, he rounded a curve and suddenly jammed on his brakes. A car was stopped in the lane, no lights on. No leeway existed on the narrow country road and John knew he'd have to risk running his truck onto the rocky, tree-lined shoulder or crash into the stopped car in front of him.

He twisted his steering wheel to the right...and prayed for the best.

His truck hit a boulder beside the road and his axle snapped when he landed on lower ground. He knew it before the truck had stopped moving. He spoke words his mother would have raised her eyebrows at, but he felt sure those words were justified.

He got out of his truck and climbed up to the road, angry now that someone had left their car on the road. Even if it had broken down, the least they could've done was push it to the side. He'd assumed no one was in the car, but when he knocked on the glass to be sure, a head popped up.

He thanked God he'd avoided the vehicle. "Can you roll down the window a little?"

The woman did so.

"Are you broken down?"

"Y-yes."

"Then why didn't you move your car off the road?"

"I—I can't."

His eyes followed her hand as she patted her stomach, and he realized she was pregnant.

Very pregnant.

"We've got to get you out of your car before another vehicle comes along and hits it."

"I don't think I can walk."

"Come on, I'll help you."

"Where will I go?"

"To my truck for the moment. I'll call for help after I get you safe and your car off the road."

"You have a cell phone?"

"Yeah." He tried to open her door. "Can you unlock your door?"

"Yes."

He got her door open and helped her out. Then he half dragged and half helped her into his truck down below.

"Just stay put while I see what I can do about your car. Do you know what's wrong with it?"

"I don't know, but it started hissing and smoke started coming out of the hood."

"Okay. I'll see if I can push it on to the shoulder. I'll be back in just a minute." At least he would if he didn't get run over on the pitch-dark road. Fortunately, he didn't expect a lot of cars at that time of night.

Changing the gear to neutral, he pushed the car to the side of the road. There wasn't that much space, but it would give anyone coming around the curve some room to maneuver.

He slid back down the gully to his truck and got in the front seat. "There, I got your car pushed to the side. Now let's see if we can rouse some help." He knew his insurance would pay for his truck, so he could be cheerful now that he'd calmed down.

Until he opened his phone.

He cursed several times and snapped his phone shut.

"What's wrong?" she asked cautiously.

"I forgot to recharge my cell."

"Do you have a charger with you?"

"No."

"Wh-what are we going to do?"

"I don't know. At least I got your car out of the way so no one else will have to wreck their car."

"Are you saying I caused your wreck?"

"You didn't even have any lights on!"

"I had them on, but my battery died!"

"Look, it's all right. My insurance will pay for it, but I can't drive it. So we'll just sit tight until someone comes along."

"I've been here for a couple of hours and you were the first one to come along. Do…do you think someone else will—"

She grimaced and grabbed her stomach.

"Is something wrong?"

She lay back against the seat, breathing deeply. "No, I just need to…stay calm."

"Just how far along are you?"

"About eight months."

That brought John up short. He sure didn't want to talk her into early labor. He agreed—calm was just what they needed.

"Look, we'll probably see someone fairly soon. Until then, tell me what you're doing on this road."

"I'm just driving."

"Toward what destination? There's not much on this road except Rawhide."

She jerked away from him.

"What did I say?"

"Nothing!"

"Okay, well, I'm from Rawhide, a small town that most of my family lives in. I'm John Randall. I run my family ranch about fifteen miles outside of town. But I have cousins all over town and on three other ranches in the area. We joke all the time because you can't go anywhere without running into one of us."

"Is it a nice town?"

"Absolutely. Both doctors, the sheriff, the only law-yer, the two accountants, all are kin to us. My sister is a jewelry designer. The drama teacher is kin to us, too. She used to be a movie star."

"M-my brother is a deputy."

John frowned. "In Rawhide?"

"Yes."

"Who is he? I bet I know him."

"I don't think I should say."

"Why not?"

"I'm not…not staying in town. I just needed to ask him s-something."

"You couldn't just call him?"

"I tried several times but—but he didn't answer his phone."

"Maybe he's on vacation. No, that couldn't be it. The only one on vacation is Harry and——"

She jerked again.

He stared at her. "Your brother is Harry? Harry Gowan?"

"Please, I didn't say that."

"Harry is my brother-in-law."

"Oh!"

"Stay calm. It's all right. Harry would want me to help you. What's wrong?"

Saying nothing, she shook her head and folded her arms over her protruding stomach, as if she were cold.

He took her by her shoulders. "Look, Harry is on——"

He broke off because she was wincing in pain. "Are you in labor?"

She shook her head.

"Then what's wrong?"

"I—I have some bruises."

He turned on the inside lights. "Take your coat off."

"I don't want to. It's cold."

"I think you need to."

"You can't see anything."

"What do you mean?"

"He didn't hit me where it could be seen."

"He who?"

"M-my husband."

"Are you saying your husband beat you?"

She nodded her head, her gaze lowered.

"Had he hit you before now?"

"Once," she whispered. "I thought he wouldn't do it again. He—he said he was sorry."

"So what happened this time?"

"He—he decided he didn't want the baby." She sobbed, then, tears streaking down her cheeks.

He scooted across the seat and wrapped his arms around her. "He's a fool!"

She buried her face against him and wept.

After a minute, she collected herself and, in spite of sniffles, said, "When he got up this morning and left for work at six, I grabbed what I could and went to the bank when it opened. I took all our money and I drove to Rawhide. At least I tried to drive to Rawhide. I hoped Harry could help me."

"He's out of town for about six weeks."

"Oh." She sniffed several times, trying to control herself.

"Look— I don't even know your name. But I can promise you I'll do what I can to help you. Remember I said the sheriff was kin to us?"

She nodded her head as it rested against his chest.

"Well, that means he's kin to you, too. Harry is his favorite deputy. He'd help you even if Harry wasn't part of the family."

"How is Harry part of your family?"

"You didn't know? Harry married my sister."

"Oh, I didn't realize— Then I can't bother Harry."

"Then what will you do?"

"Can my car be fixed?"

"Yeah, if Larry can get the parts. That could take a week. Then he'll take about a week to fix it."

"How do you know?"

"I'm guessing you knocked a hole in your radiator."

"Oh."

"Hey, you can stay at our house while they work on your car."

"No." That was all she said.

"What's your name?" he asked, which seemed a silly question since he was holding her in his arms.

"Lucy."

"Well, Lucy, take off your coat."

"Why?" She pulled back and fear lit her eyes when she looked at him.

"I'm going to wrap us up in a comforter I have so we can stay warm until morning."

She scanned the truck. "You have a comforter?"

"Sure. It's not safe to drive around here without something to keep us warm."

"Where is it?"

"You don't believe me, do you?"

"I just want to see it first."

He took his arms from around her and scooted across the front seat until he could reach in the back. He had to stretch to take hold of the comforter, and a bottle of Gatorade. He brought them to the front seat.

Her eyes widened when she saw the drink. "Um, I'm really thirsty."

"I don't have any cups, but I think we can both share it." He took off the lid and offered her a drink. Then he took one himself.

"Now will you take off your coat?"

"Wouldn't we be warmer if we kept our coats on?"

"No. Body heat will keep us warmer. Besides, it's not going to get that cold tonight."

He took off his coat and laid it aside. Then he waited for her to do the same. Once she did, he spread the comforter over both of them and drew her back into his arms.

"You've got to relax, Lucy," he coaxed, feeling how rigid she was against him.

"I—I'm not sure I can."

"Sure you can. I know, I'll tell you stories about Harry. That should make you feel better." He began telling her things Harry had done, particularly the humorous ones. Finally he felt her relax against his chest.

After a few minutes of her silence, he whispered her name.

All he heard in response was the deep, steady breathing of a woman who had fallen asleep. He breathed in her scent. It reminded him of a fragrant blue flower that grew on the mountainside in spring.

He eased her even closer to him and lay his head against the headrest. His last thought was how right she felt in his arms.

Lucy came awake suddenly. She was snugly warm in her sleeping rescuer's arms, but, unfortunately, she needed to go to the bathroom. She tried to slide out from under the comforter, but he stirred.

"What's wrong?" he whispered.

She was embarrassed to tell him, but she had no choice.

"Oh, okay, let's put on our coats."

"No! I mean, you don't have to… I'll be all right on my own."

"Lucy, I'm not going to watch you. But you'll need help getting down. I'll help you and then I'll walk around the truck so you're out of sight."

"All right."

He put on his coat and handed her hers. Then he stepped over her and got out of the truck. She shivered as she followed him down.

"It's really cold," she said with chattering teeth.

"Yeah, so let's hurry. You should be all right here. I'll go around to the front of the truck."

He stood there in the cold, staring out at the night, waiting for her to call him. When she finally did, he came around the truck and helped her back in. "Okay, let's shed our coats and huddle up again."

This time he didn't have to urge her to get close or to relax. She went naturally back into his arms and he spread the comforter over both of them.

Gradually they both warmed up and she relaxed against his chest.

"John?"

"Yeah?" he asked, on the verge of falling asleep again.

"Thank you."

"For what?"

"For taking care of me."

"No problem," he told her. Together they'd managed very well, better than he would've done alone. He settled her more comfortably against his chest.

He checked his watch. It was almost two o'clock. They still had a good portion of the night to get through.

They both went back to sleep.

Just as dawn broke, they both awakened because of sudden moisture. John assumed Lucy had had an accident. Lucy, however, thought something else had happened.

"I think my water broke."

"What?" he asked groggily.

"I think my water broke. That means I'll be going into labor soon."

His eyes flew open. "You're what? But we can't— I mean, how soon will you— How much time do we have?"

"I don't know!" She sounded frightened.

He felt the same way, but he realized he had to be the calm one. "It's all right. Daylight is breaking. Someone will come along soon enough."

"Are—are you sure?"

"Yeah. I'm sure, and if not, then we'll manage."

"Have you ever delivered a baby before?"

"Nope. But I've delivered calves and foals. It's almost the same, I'm sure."

"I'm sorry you— I mean, I'm sorry this is happening. I'm so embarrassed!"

"Don't be, Lucy. Having a child is a natural thing."

"You're so comforting, John. I don't think I would've made it if you hadn't stopped."

He considered how he'd stopped his truck and decided not to mention it again. Lucy couldn't help what had happened and she'd had a pretty rough time of it.

Lucy grabbed his shirt and gasped.

"What is it?" he asked.

"I think I'm in labor now!"

"What did you feel?"

"A tightening along the bottom of my stomach."

He cleared his throat. Calmly he said, "That sounds about right, but it will probably be a while before anything happens."

He hoped to God he was right. He lifted his wrist so he could read his watch. It was ten until six.

When Lucy woke him again, he checked his watch. It was almost six-thirty. He felt sure that was good. A weak sun was providing a little more warmth, and he realized he'd need to get out of the truck to see if he could flag down a car so they could get help.

"Okay, Lucy, I'm going to get near the road so I can flag down a car. You'll be all right here under the blanket. Okay?"

"I don't want you to go."

"How else will we get help?" He laughed slightly. "Believe me, I'd rather stay here with you."

"Can't you wait a little while?"

"Yeah, okay. I'll wait until seven."

"Thank you. I know I'm being too clingy, but—but you're so comforting."

"You're not clingy. I just want to take care of you, Lucy. It's important to get you to the hospital before anything happens."

"First babies are supposed to take a long time."

"Okay. We'll just stay where we are for a little bit longer."

To John's surprise, he went to sleep again, as did Lucy. He awoke at eight o'clock, long after his normal time. Lucy was still sleeping against him. He smiled down at her. He guessed her labor wasn't as imminent as it had sounded at six.

He tried to open the glove box without disturbing her, knowing he had several packets of peanut butter crackers in there. He was hungry. Of course he would save a packet for Lucy. Unfortunately, she woke up.

Her eyes flew open and she looked around frantically for a moment. Then she settled down as she realized where she was.

"Are you hungry?" he asked her. "I think I have a couple of packets of peanut butter crackers."

"Where?"

"In the glove box. Can you reach them?"

"Yes." She opened the glove box and found the packets. She handed them both to John.

"Don't you want one?"

"I've heard that you shouldn't eat if you're in labor."

"I don't think that would hurt anything. Take a packet."

"All right."

They unwrapped the crackers and ate them slowly.

Lucy had only eaten one when she tensed again. "It's another pain."

"All right." He checked his watch. It was eight-twenty.

"I'll wait until you feel another one. Then I'll go up on the road and try to flag someone down."

"Okay."

"Eat the rest of your crackers. You'll need them."

She ate slowly, trying to make them last.

John brought out the Gatorade again for them each to have a drink.

When the next pain came so soon, it surprised them both. John checked his watch again. It wasn't eight-thirty yet. The pains were coming faster.

"Don't go, John. Please."

"I have to. We've got to get you to a hospital."

"But you said we'd be all right."

"We will be, if we have to deliver your baby here, but I'd prefer a hospital. Now, be strong. I'm going to cover you back up and I'll be back as soon as I can."

"You aren't going to leave, are you? I mean, walk somewhere?"

"No. That would take too long."

"Okay."

He tucked her in and got out of the truck. After climbing up to the road, he paced back and forth in front of her car, hoping someone would come by.

He almost gave up and decided to go back down to his truck to see how Lucy was doing, but at the last minute, he heard a vehicle approaching.

Stepping farther out into the road, he waved his arms as the pickup came into sight.

"You break down?" the man asked, after lowering his window.

"Yeah, and I've got a woman in labor down there."

"All right. I'm going as far as Rawhide. Will that help?"

"That's where we need to go. I'll just go bring her up."

"Need some help?"

"No, I've got her."

John slid back down to the truck and opened the passenger door. "Lucy, we've got a ride."

She looked up at him and he saw the pain on her face. "Thank God. This baby wants to be born."

Chapter Two

John scooped Lucy up in his arms, comforter and all.

"My coat!"

He grabbed it and laid it across her so she could keep it from falling. "Do you have suitcases?"

"Yes, in my trunk."

"Get out your keys. I'll stop and put them in his truck before we get in."

"Wouldn't it be better for me to get in and then put the suitcases in? He might drive off with them."

"I'd rather he drive off with your suitcases than with you."

"I hadn't thought of that."

He brought her out of the truck and struggled up to the road. Then he set her down for a minute to deal with her luggage. Next, he scooped Lucy up again and set her on the car seat, pushing her over so he could get in, too.

Before he shut the door, the driver took off, as if he were trying to leave John behind. Lucy shrieked and John used the door handle to hang on until he could get his footing inside the truck.

Then he sent the man a sharp look.

"Figured you was in a hurry, what with the baby comin' and all."

"Yeah." Under his breath he added, "But not in that big of a hurry."

After several minutes of seeing how the man drove, John wasn't sure he'd improved their status any. The man was driving eighty miles an hour and taking up most of the road.

John hated to ask the question, but for Lucy's sake, he needed to. "Do you happen to have a cell phone?"

"Sure do. Want to borrow it?"

"Yeah. I'll be glad to pay you for your minutes."

"Okay."

John dialed the number for the clinic. "May I speak to Caro, please?"

"Dr. Randall is in with a patient."

"Is Jon?"

"Yes, he is."

"Look, go tell Caro I have a pregnant woman who thinks she's going into labor and I need to talk to her."

He didn't have to wait long for Caroline to come to the phone. "Who is this?"

"It's John. Sorry I forgot to tell the nurse that."

"That's all right. Your message sounded urgent."

"Yeah. Lucy's water broke about six. Her pains have been coming about ten minutes apart and she thinks she's eight months pregnant."

"Where are you?"

"A kind gentleman is giving us a ride. We should be there in about forty minutes."

"Okay, you should arrive before she delivers, but you don't have much time to spare. With the baby coming early we'll need to get it oxygen right away."

"Yes."

"She can hear you?"

"Yes."

"Can you tell me how you came across this woman?"

"No."

"Is she from around here?"

"No."

"Well, John, you've got my curiosity up. We'll be waiting for both of you, and we'll have an incubator ready, too."

"Thanks, Caro."

"No problem. Do you want me to call your parents?"

"Yeah, just tell them I'm all right. I'll talk to them later."

"All right. I will."

When John handed the phone back to the driver, he looked at John. "That'll be twenty dollars."

John didn't question the amount. He dug in his pocket for his wallet and pulled out a twenty-dollar bill. He handed it over without argument.

"How are you doing?" he asked Lucy.

"I think my pains are coming faster."

"Caro said we should have plenty of time to get you to the clinic. She'll take care of everything."

"Who is she?"

"She's my cousin, one of the doctors in town."

"Oh, so she knows about having babies."

"Yep. She's had a couple herself."

"Who is her husband?"

"The sheriff."

"You know the sheriff?" the old man asked, suddenly interested.

"Yes."

"He's the one I'm goin' to see!"

"That's good. I'll show you where his office is."

"Okay."

Lucy gasped as another pain, more intense this time, seized her.

"Try to relax, Lucy. I know it's hard, but we'll be there soon." He put his arm around her, still enveloped in the comforter. Her scent wafted to his nose and in his mind he was back in his truck spending the night with Lucy wrapped in his arms.

"You two live in Rawhide?"

John squeezed Lucy's shoulder, forgetting about her pain until she grimaced again. "Yes, we do."

"Nice place. I was gonna settle down there, but I didn't. I heard about the sheriff, though. They say he does right by people."

"Yes, he does."

"Yeah, I'm gonna talk to him."

"You got a problem with someone in Rawhide?" John asked.

"Yeah!"

"I know a lot of people in Rawhide. Maybe I know who you have a problem with."

"I don't think so."

"I might."

"Nope."

John gave up the puzzle of the stranger. He didn't really care about him as long as he got them to the hospital in time. And they didn't have much time left. He felt Lucy trying to relax, but the pain came even harder than the last time. He checked his watch surreptitiously, noting the time was nine-twenty-nine. The last pain had been at nine-twenty-one. He didn't say anything to Lucy. And he certainly didn't want to urge the old man to drive faster.

But he hoped they got there soon.

When they passed the turn to his family ranch, he smiled. At this speed, they were five minutes away.

"Uh, you'd better slow down inside the city limits. You don't want to meet the sheriff from the back of a squad car."

"I guess you're right."

"Can't we just tell him we have an emergency?" Lucy asked.

"Good thinking, girl," the driver said as he accelerated. "That'll do it!"

They got pulled over two minutes later, just as they entered the town.

The deputy pulled behind them and approached the car. "Pardon me, sir, but did you know you were going eighty miles an—"

"Dave," John interrupted him, leaning toward the driver's window, "we're trying to get to the hospital. She's in labor." He nodded toward Lucy.

The deputy sprang to action. "I'll lead the way!"

John laughed under his breath. There was no traffic

on Rawhide's main road, but now the deputy was turning on his siren and motioning for them to follow him. It was a little ridiculous, but John didn't suggest the driver slow down again.

He noticed Mike coming out of his office to find out what the siren was for. He'd come to the hospital to talk to his wife.

The squad car came to a halt beside the clinic and the old man pulled right in behind it.

"Thank you so much for helping us." John started easing Lucy out of the truck.

"You aren't going to pay for the gas?" the driver asked.

Lucy stared at the man, but John reached for his billfold again. "I guess that would be twenty dollars again, wouldn't it?"

"Well, it might a' been more, but I'll let you slide, seein' as you're having a little one."

"Thanks."

"Don't forget my luggage," Lucy reminded him.

Since two nurses were bringing a gurney down the slanted sidewalk and Lucy would be cared for, he reached in for the luggage. Then he followed Lucy and the nurses into the clinic.

"John?" Lucy called, holding her hand out to him. "Will you—will you mind going in with me? I—I'm scared."

"Yeah, I'll go in with you, Lucy."

"Thank you so much."

He grinned. "I guess that will be twenty dollars, right?"

She smiled back. "That man would've charged us for breathing if he could figure out how."

"Probably. I was just glad I had enough twenties to last us. I think he would've thrown us out if I hadn't."

"He kept staring at my stomach, as if I were faking labor to get a ride."

"You are having pains, aren't you?" the nurse asked.

"Yes. The last one was— What time was it, John?"

"Nine-twenty-nine."

"How far apart are they?" the nurse asked.

"About— Ohhh… Now!"

"But it's only nine-thirty-five!" John said as he looked at his watch. He yelled out, "Caro! She's down to six minutes apart and coming faster."

A tall woman in a white medical coat came out of her office.

"Hello. I'm Dr. Randall. I haven't met you, have I?"

"No. I—I'm Lucy."

"Well, welcome to our little hospital. John said you were eight months along?"

"Yes."

"Okay, my nurses are going to take you in this room, so I can do a quick examination."

"John?" Lucy cried urgently.

"Caro, I think she'll be more calm if I go with her."

"Of course, John. If you stand by her head, you won't be in the way and you won't see anything."

John did as Caroline suggested. Lucy clutched his hand as if it was a magic charm. He bent and added a kiss to her hand.

Caroline gave John a sharp look. But he didn't say

anything. Lucy was frightened and he wanted to re-assure her as much as he could.

After a quick examination, Caroline stood up and told the nurse to bring in the sonogram machine. "Lucy, we're going to look at your baby on our sonogram machine. That means I'll need to put some jelly on your tummy."

"John can stay, can't he?"

"Certainly. We always let the father stay if he wants."

John didn't correct her assumption, nor did Lucy say anything.

Caroline raised her top for the ultrasound and the purple bruises on her stomach were obvious.

"Lucy, who beat you?" Caroline asked.

"M-my husband."

"John? John did this?"

Caroline was shocked, and John hurried to reassure her. "No. No, I didn't do this."

"Then who?"

"My husband," Lucy said again.

"Where is he?"

"Kansas City…I hope."

"Was he trying to cause a miscarriage?"

"I think so." Tears slid down her cheeks, and John bent down to reassure her.

"All right, let's do the sonogram. I have to press down a little, but considering what you've withstood, I think you'll be all right." Caroline spread the jelly over Lucy's stomach and then she pressed a roller on her stomach connected to the machine.

"Now you can see your baby. There's so much

natural insulation I think she's survived and is doing fine."

"It's a girl?" Lucy asked, holding her breath.

"Yes. I think you may be a little further along than eight months. I think your baby is going to come about two weeks early. She might even be six pounds."

"Is that good?"

"It means you can take her home after a couple of days."

Lucy closed her eyes and tears rolled down her cheeks.

John knew the problem immediately. He bent down to whisper to her, "Don't cry, Lucy. You can come home with me. I'll be holding your hand all the way. Okay? We'll give your baby a home. It will be all right."

John's words didn't give her the reassurance she needed. Sobs ripped out of her as she lost control.

"Lucy, what's wrong?" Caroline asked.

She just shook her head. John put his arms around her and brought her face to his chest, turning her toward him. "It's all right. We're going to take care of you, both of you."

"I can't s-stay, John. He'll find me," she said between sobs.

"Are you talking about the man who beat you up— your husband?" Caroline asked, her voice turning hard.

"I need to go away!" Lucy sniffed and then gasped as another pain hit her.

"Honey, right now you have to have a baby. You

can deal with the other things afterward." John held her close.

Caroline ordered the nurse to bring Lucy into the delivery room then turned to John.

"We're going to change her into a hospital gown. If she doesn't mind, you can go in."

"Maybe I'd better step outside until they get you changed, Lucy, but I won't go anywhere, I promise."

"You'll come right back?" Lucy asked, her hand still clinging to him.

"Yes, I promise."

"We'll call you, John," the nurse told him.

He moved out into the hall, and Caroline was waiting for him. She didn't look too pleased. "What is going on here?"

He lowered his eyes. "I don't think she wants me to tell you."

"Well, you're going to have to explain to your parents. They think they're here to see the birth of your child."

His head shot up. "Why would they think that?"

"Because you've brought a lady to town who's pregnant and you're going into the examination room with her, just like a husband."

"No, that's not it. I can't—"

"John, she wants you back in there with her," the nurse said.

He turned back to Caro. "Tell them I'll be out to talk to them later. Okay?"

"Whatever you say. How's she doing, Wendy?"

"The pains are coming faster, Doctor."

John interrupted the nurse's report. "I'm going

back in with her, Caro. I'll stay at her head and just try to keep her calm."

"All right, John. I'll go talk to your parents."

"It's not what they're thinking. She's…almost family."

"Yeah, right!" Caroline said as she headed out to the waiting area.

John wanted to go to his parents, but he'd promised Lucy he'd be there for her. He'd explain to them later. He entered the delivery room to find Lucy still sobbing. Immediately taking her hand, John kissed it and stroked it, then put his arm around her.

With his deep voice, he talked to Lucy, calming her as he had earlier. "Hey, Lucy, we made it to the hospital. That's a good thing, don't you think? Now you can be sure your baby will get good care. That beats a comforter in a pickup truck, doesn't it?"

"I'm so glad you're here, John," Lucy said, her voice weaker as she tried to bear the pain.

"I'm glad, too. You're going to be fine."

The nurse entered then. "All right, Lucy, I'm going to give you a shot that should relieve some of the pain. Just hold still."

"She'll be all right?" John asked, looking for reassurance.

"Yes, she'll be fine. We just like to make it a little easier." She gave the injection then she said, "Okay, Lucy, just draw a deep breath. You'll find it's more bearable now."

John lost track of time as he stood by Lucy, watching her suffer for the sake of her child. He hadn't had firsthand experience of a child being born and had no idea what a woman went through to give birth. To think that Lucy's husband had tried to provoke a miscarriage just broke John's heart.

When Caro came in, called by the nurse, John knew it was time. He wanted to let Lucy rest, to take a well-deserved break, but he knew she had more work ahead of her.

Several pushes later Lucy let out a gutteral groan and gave birth to her daughter. When Caro held Lucy's baby in her arms and they all heard that fierce cry, John could feel tears in his eyes.

"You did it, Lucy!" he said, bending down to envelop her in a hug. "You did it!"

Lucy looked relieved. "Can I see her?"

"Yes, as soon as the nurses clean her up," Caro replied. "She's got all her fingers and toes and looks like she's healthy. After you see her, I'll do an examination."

"Thank you so much, Doctor. I'm so happy."

John realized he shared Lucy's happiness. Because she was Harry's sister, of course. That was the only reason…wasn't it?

When he considered that he had to face his parents, he realized he needed to be able to reveal Lucy's identity. He knew his mother would take Lucy under her wing like a mother hen, if she knew. And he had to be able to put Lucy there. Once they were alone, he'd talk to her about revealing her identity.

The nurses brought Lucy's baby back into the room. Caroline took the baby in her arms and carried her to Lucy. "Here's your little girl, Lucy."

Lucy held her baby in her arms, glowing at the tiny creature.

"John, look!"

"She's a beauty, sweetheart."

As Lucy began to fade a little from the exhilaration, John reached out and took the baby from her. As he felt the warmth of the baby, the little life, he stared in amazement.

Caroline took the baby from him. "I need to examine her now, John. I think Lucy is going to sleep. A well-deserved rest, I might add."

He nodded. "I'll stay with her until she falls sleep."

"All right, but don't forget your parents are waiting for an explanation."

"No, I won't."

Once Lucy was back in a room, John waited until the nurse had left before he broached the subject of her identity. "Lucy, I need to explain to my parents about you being Harry's sister. You understand that, don't you?"

She nodded, as if resigned. Then reality struck and Lucy's features crumpled. John knew she'd come face-to-face with the reality of not having a home for her baby.

"Lucy, Mom will take you in, you and the baby. I live with my parents, so I'll be there, too."

"I can't stay there, John. I'm afraid he'll come find me. He—he's threatened me before about leaving him. He told me he'd come after me if I left him."

"Honey, we won't let him hurt you or the baby. I promise."

"But I don't want to bring trouble to either you or Harry. It doesn't seem fair."

"We won't worry about that, Lucy. Your husband is a coward. Only a coward would attack a pregnant woman, any woman, much less his own."

"I want to file for divorce as soon as I can. But I don't feel I can bring trouble down on you. Please don't ask me to—"

"Honey, I'm telling you, you can't deny your baby a home. That's what I'm telling you."

Caroline came into Lucy's room, a little bundle in her arms. "Lucy, your baby is as healthy as can be. And she weighs six pounds, one ounce. She'll be able to go home with you."

John took Lucy's hand and held it in his own. "Lucy, you need to tell Caro who you are," he said, hoping to force Lucy to reveal her identity.

"No, John!" Lucy protested.

"You know you need to. I'm going to have to tell my parents, too."

Ignoring him, Lucy held out her arms for her baby. "Can I hold her?"

Caroline handed the tiny infant to her mother. "I need to know her name, Lucy."

"Oh, I want to name her after my grandmother. Emma."

"That's a lovely name. Now, what's her last name?"

Keeping her head down, Lucy said, "Horton."

"All right. Do you have a middle name?"

"I think Lynn. Emma Lynn Horton."

"That's lovely."

John wasn't satisfied. "Tell her, Lucy!

"No!"

"You must. For Emma's sake."

Caroline remained silent, but he could feel her eyes on him.

"You must," John prompted Lucy again. "Tell her why I said you were family."

Finally, Lucy raised her head and looked at Caroline. "I'm Harry Gowan's sister."

Chapter Three

"You're Harry's sister?" Caro seemed pleasantly surprised. "How did you come to know John?"

"I didn't know him till yesterday. But he's been so very kind to me. I'll never be able to thank him adequately." She looked at John, gratitude in her eyes. "I was alone and scared and he made me feel safe. He even convinced me he could deliver my baby."

Caroline stared at John. "Oh, really?"

"I was just trying to reassure her. I'm not challenging your skills, Caroline. You know that. But we were both stranded on the road last night, and all we could hope for was a car to stop by so we could get a ride into town."

"But I don't understand how you got together. Did you—"

"I'll tell you later. I think Lucy should get some sleep."

"All right," Caroline agreed. She knew Lucy was exhausted. "Let me take the baby. I'll put her in a bassinet."

"Thank you," Lucy said.

As Caro exited with Emma, John told her, "I'll stay with Lucy until she falls asleep. Then I'll go talk to my parents."

"Are you going to leave then, John?" Lucy asked.

He heard the fear in her voice, and he said, "No, I won't leave you, Lucy. My parents are waiting here. I'll just visit them for a little bit while you sleep."

"I know I'm being a baby about you staying. I promise I'll get stronger, but right now I can't quite be brave."

"You don't have to. I'm here." He took her hand in his and insisted she go to sleep. After several minutes, he slipped his hand away and waited to see if she would wake up. When she didn't, he left the room. In the hallway, he found a nurse. "I'm going to the waiting room to talk to my parents. Let me know if she wakes up."

"Okay. Do you want to take the baby to show them?"

"Can I do that?"

"Caro said you could."

"Yeah, I'd like that."

John figured his parents would like to see the baby. His mother would be excited about the tiny infant, and his father's protective urge would be aroused.

Besides, he liked holding Emma.

When he reached the waiting room, he saw his parents sitting quietly. He stepped into the room, holding Emma, and his parents jumped to their feet. He couldn't help the proud smile he wore. "I want to introduce you to Emma," he said, pulling the blanket back a little.

"Oh! Let me hold her," Camille Randall said.

He immediately handed the baby to her. He and his father crowded around. It was amazing to him that his parents didn't demand an explanation. But he would give them one anyway. "I'm not the father."

Griff Randall looked at him sharply. "Then who is?"

"A man named Cecil. The important person of the two who created this baby is the mother."

"Who is she?"

"She's Harry's sister."

"What?" Camille said. She appeared stunned.

"I said she's Harry's sister."

"But how did you know her?" his father asked.

John replayed the past twelve hours for his parents. "She's scared and doesn't know what to do. Her husband beat her, hoping to provoke a miscarriage."

Horrified, his parents stared at the infant in Camille's arms.

"Oh, no!" Camille said, holding the baby closer.

"We'll protect her and her child, of course," Griff said.

John realized how wonderful his parents were. He felt sure they would've said the same thing if Lucy wasn't Harry's sister, but he was glad there was a family connection.

"I know I'm supposed to be running the ranch, Dad, but could you fill in for a day or two? Lucy feels alone right now. I can give her some assurance that she and her baby are safe."

"I'm sure Harry would appreciate that, John," Griff said. "I can take care of the ranch for a few days."

"Thanks, Dad. And, Mom, I told Lucy she and the baby could come to the ranch at least until Harry got back."

"Well, of course they can. She can take your sister's old room and the baby can go in the one next door. It'll be perfect. I'll get started fixing it up this afternoon."

"Don't go to extremes, Mom. I don't think Emma will know the difference and Lucy will just be grateful to be safe."

"No, I won't. I bet she hasn't gotten any baby things for Emma. She likely wouldn't since she was on the run. I can make those arrangements, too."

"All right, but don't overwhelm her. She's not used to a family like ours."

"Oh, no, just the necessities for this little darling." Camille looked down at the baby sleeping in her arms. "She's almost like my own grandbaby. What about Lucy's parents?"

"Harry told me they got divorced a long time ago. Lucy didn't mention either of them."

"Then we'll be this little girl's grandparents, at least for a little while."

"Let me hold her a minute," Griff said, reaching for the pink bundle. He peeled back the blanket to get a good look at her. "Isn't she beautiful?"

"Yeah," John agreed. "Caro says if she holds her own, she can go home with Lucy."

"How much did she weigh?" Camille asked.

"Six pounds one ounce."

"Oh, yes, she'll need to grow a little." She cooed at

the baby, "Listen, little Emma, you drink all your milk so you'll weigh a little more. Then you can come home with your mommy."

"You think she heard you, Mom?"

"You never know, John. Babies understand a lot more than we might think."

"Okay, I'd better take her back to her mother, in case Lucy wakes up and thinks her baby is missing. I'm not sure when I'll be home, Dad. Thanks for taking over for me."

"No problem. We'll call it family leave."

John was smiling as he carried Emma back to her bassinet. She stretched in his arms, as if she was trying to grow. "Not too fast, Emma. You need to be a baby for a little longer. That way you can have lots of cuddling."

When he reached the room, Lucy was asleep and he settled Emma in her own small bed to sleep alongside her mother.

When he came out of Lucy's room, Caroline caught him. "Mike wants to talk to you. He said he could come here if that would help."

"Yeah, it would. Shall I call him?"

"I'll let him know."

"Okay, I'll be in the waiting room."

After letting Lucy's nurse know where he'd be, he settled on one of the sofas in the waiting room, glad his parents had gone home. At least now they knew he hadn't brought a woman pregnant with his child to the hospital as a surprise. But he almost wished Lucy was his woman. She seemed so gentle and caring and…lost. He felt a need to be responsible for her.

Mike walked into the waiting room. He must've driven down to get there this fast.

"Did that old man talk to you?"

Mike came to an abrupt halt. "Did you have something to do with that?"

"He's the one who brought us to town."

"I didn't know that. But I wanted to talk to you about the woman you brought in."

"Didn't Caro tell you?"

"Tell me what?"

"Who she is. She's Harry's sister."

Mike stared at him blankly. "You're kidding."

"No, I'm not."

"Did you ask her for proof?"

"No, I didn't. I'm not a lawman."

"Damn it, John, you can't just take her word for it."

"Do you know her married name? I don't. Well, I do now, but I didn't then."

"Maybe her driver's license has her maiden name on it. A lot of women do that, for some reason."

"Do you want me to go get her purse? I know where it is. I'll be back in a minute." John felt kind of bad about getting Lucy's wallet while she was sleeping, but Mike had to see the proof.

When he came out, Caroline was talking with her husband.

"Why didn't you tell me she'd been beaten, John?"

"Hell, you wouldn't even believe who she is without proof. I figured we should prove her identity to you before we discussed what she'd been through."

"Caro just told me about her bruises."

"Yeah, and I took her by the shoulders and she winced. She said she was bruised there, too. When I told her to take off her coat so I could see, she said he didn't hit her where other people could see."

"Sounds like a pro."

"She said he only hit her one other time, and he apologized and told her it wouldn't happen again."

"Did she say why he beat her this time?"

"She said he didn't want the baby…and then she broke down in sobs."

"Poor thing," Caroline said. "Being pregnant is hard enough when both of you want the baby. When one of you doesn't, it's nearly unbearable. To have him try to destroy her baby is inhuman."

Mike Davis put his arm around his wife. They'd been thrilled with both their children, but Mike knew she felt a lot of sympathy toward women who suffered at the hands of their husbands.

"What's she going to do?" Caroline asked.

"I talked to Mom and Dad and they're willing to welcome her to our house. Mom was planning what she would do to make them happy."

"And she agreed to do that?"

"I haven't actually talked to her about it. She thinks she should go away where her husband won't find her. But she doesn't know where to go. That's why she was calling Harry. But he didn't answer."

"No, he's on vacation, but I think he'd want us to help her. We could take her if you can't," Mike said.

John grinned. "Mom would never forgive me if she got away."

"You do realize her husband might come after her."

"Yeah. If he does, we'll call you, Mike, but Dad and I will be ready."

"Good. The MO of these kind of men is to keep hitting their wives. They don't stop at two beatings. I'm glad she got out."

"Me, too."

"When you talk to Harry, tell him we've got the situation covered."

"I will, Mike. He'll know he can rely on both of us. And Mom is so excited. She's looking forward to having a baby in the house again."

"Are you going to stay available until she settles down? She seems to need reassurance for a while," Caroline said.

"Yeah, I'm going to stay here until she's okay with everything. I may stay until she can leave. Dad has offered to handle any problems with the ranch until I bring her and the baby home."

"I just want to warn you, John, that her emotions will be all over the place. It happens after childbirth." Caroline studied him and John dropped his gaze.

"I'm just offering protection, like Harry would want me to do."

Mike clapped him on his back. "All right, we've got everything squared away for now. When she's doing better, we'll ask her if she'll file charges."

When he left, John went back to Lucy's room, wondering if either of the ladies he was in charge of would be awake. A nurse was changing Emma's diaper and he asked if the baby had woken up.

"Yes, we had the intercom on so she wouldn't wake up her mother. She's going to take a bottle."

"Can I feed it to her?"

"Sure. You'll have to coax her to eat but usually babies catch on pretty quickly. I'll wait and see if she does."

"Great." He slid his hand beneath the baby and lifted her against his chest. "Hey, little girl, you get a bottle so you can grow. Will you be a good girl and eat it all?"

With blue eyes like her mother the baby stared at him as if he were saying something important.

The nurse handed John the bottle and he tried to insert the nipple in Emma's mouth. After a moment, he succeeded. When she chewed down on the nipple, she realized she would get a reward.

Suddenly, John didn't have any more trouble. Little Emma greedily sucked the bottle dry.

The nurse, who had waited to see how John would do, told him to burp Emma on his shoulder. He put the baby on his shoulder and patted her back as the nurse instructed.

When he did, Emma let out a most unladylike burp. He stared down at her. "Was that you, Emma? My, you did that well."

The nurse laughed. "That happens with some babies. She did just fine. Now put her back in her bassinet and she'll go to sleep."

"She will?"

The nurse nodded.

He gently laid the baby back in her bed. She squirmed and wiggled several times and then went to sleep.

"You did a good job," the nurse said.

"Thanks."

After she left, he eased down in the soft chair beside the bed and leaned his head back, suddenly tired. It was more comfortable than the truck last night. But now he didn't get to hold Lucy.

LUCY STRUGGLED TO WAKE UP. It seemed there was something she should do, but she couldn't remember what. She put her hand on her stomach to make sure the baby was okay.

Her eyes popped open. Her womb didn't feel as though her baby was there. She sat up, breathing hard. What had happened?

Then she remembered she'd had the baby, her little girl, and everything was all right.

She saw the baby sleeping in a little bassinet. She leaned back in her bed. Then she looked to the right and saw John asleep in the chair beside her bed.

He'd stayed.

He'd promised he would. But she didn't know if he'd keep his word. Now she knew he had. She rested against her pillow, studying him. He was a handsome man. But more important than that, he'd taken care of her, protected her and given her hope that she might be safe. She knew that that wasn't true, but for a short time he'd given her something she desperately needed.

What should she do now? She knew she shouldn't stay in one place for long. Cecil could find her. And he knew where Harry lived.

John had said Harry wouldn't return for six weeks, which meant she was on her own. As much as she had relied on John, she couldn't any longer.

She decided her first chore was to get up and go to the bathroom. Sitting on the side of her bed, she gathered her courage and put her feet to the floor. When she stood, she almost fell, grabbing the side of the bed.

"This is harder than it looked," she muttered to herself. It wasn't that far to her initial goal. Forcing herself to move, she tottered to the bathroom, grabbing anything to give herself balance. The return trip wasn't much better. She collapsed on the bed, relieved as she settled back on the pillows. Recovery was important, she knew, but she wanted to rest a bit before she tried to get up again.

"Lucy? Are you all right?" John asked, surprising her.

"Yes, I just made the trip to the bathroom. But I didn't intend to wake you up."

"I was just napping, waiting for you to wake up. I fed Emma a bottle earlier. She did a good job."

"I hope I get to feed her the next one. I haven't done that yet."

"You will, Lucy. I took her to show to my parents, also. They fell in love with little Emma."

"That's very nice of them."

"Mom has it all arranged. She's giving you my sister's old room and there's a little room next door for Emma."

"No! No, John, I can't move in with your family. It would be too dangerous. M-My husband may come after me."

"I know that, Lucy. My dad and I will protect you, and Mike—the sheriff—came down to the hospital to assure you of his protection, too. You'll be safe with us."

"I can't do that, John. You've given me so much support when I needed it, but I can't continue to rely on you."

"What do you think you're going to do? Go back on the road? Your car won't work without a new radiator, and Emma is too little to be out on the road. You can't recover that quickly, either."

"I don't know what I'll do, but...I couldn't live with myself if I brought trouble on your head."

"You don't know the trouble you'll cause if you take Emma away from my mother." John grinned at her. "She's been wanting a grandbaby so badly. They thought I'd hidden my girlfriend's pregnancy until today."

"Oh, no! John, I'm so sorry! I didn't mean to cause you so much trouble."

"Lucy," he said, standing and moving to the bed so he could touch her. "Calm down. Mom and Dad weren't upset. Well, they might have been upset for keeping such a thing secret, but that didn't mean they wouldn't welcome my baby or her mother, if that were true."

"But surely they were disappointed in you."

"No, they're not that way. And they're happy to welcome you and Emma into the family. Like I said, Mom's rearranging so you'll be welcome."

"John, I can't stay here. I think my husband will

come after me. I don't want you to suffer because you took pity on me."

"You're not thinking clearly. You can't run all your life. That would be terrible for Emma. Stand and fight now, where you've got support. It's the only way."

"I'm not sure."

"It's what Harry would tell you. He'll be back in six weeks. Don't run away before he returns, Lucy. Surely you can stay that long."

The nurse walked in then with two lunch trays and put them on Lucy's table. "Here's your tray, too, John."

"Thanks, Heidi," John said.

Lucy looked at him after the nurse went back out. "Why do you get a tray? I mean, I think it's great but I've never been in a hospital like this one."

"Yeah, I told you everyone's great in Rawhide." He lifted the cover and took a sniff. "Mmm, we're eating well today. Fried chicken from the café."

"You mean a café provides the meals?"

"That's right. Eat all your food so you can gain some weight. You need to get stronger."

"I will. It's so nice to have someone make my meals. If I were home, I wouldn't get any food unless I prepared it."

"Don't worry. Mom will take good care of you."

"No! I'll cook and clean for her. If I go there, I can do things to make life easier for her."

John smiled at Lucy. "Whatever you can get her to let you do is fine, Lucy, but your first job is to take care of Emma. And share her a little with my mom and dad."

"Of course, if they want to see her," Lucy said, sounding unsure of that.

John sighed. "Weren't you listening to me, Lucy? They're so excited to have a baby in the house. It's going to be just fine."

Lucy still worried.

"Eat your dinner before it gets cold," John said, handing her a chicken leg.

She took his advice, knowing she needed to get her strength back. But, she wondered, when the time came, could she stay and fight?

Chapter Four

"Ready to go home, Lucy?" John asked as he entered her hospital room. He'd left her alone last night while he went back to the house to shower and get a good night's sleep, but he'd been anxious to be with her again.

"I—I'm ready to leave the hospital, John, but are you sure I should move into your parents' house? Babies aren't always quiet."

John grinned. He could imagine his mother's reaction if he should ask such a question. "I'm sure, Lucy. Mom would never forgive me if I didn't bring you there. And don't worry about Emma's crying. That's music to Mom's ears."

"But your dad?"

"He's an even bigger sucker for a baby's cry. Emma will be truly spoiled."

Lucy gave him a wistful look. "They sound lovely. I'm not sure that— I mean, I know Emma deserves the best, but—but I might irritate them." She pleaded with her eyes for him to reassure her.

"No, Lucy, you're as sweet and gentle as Emma.

There won't be a problem." John bent to place a kiss on Lucy's brow. He'd rather kiss her lips, but he was afraid he'd frighten her. She gave him another of those sad smiles that tugged at his heart.

He moved over to Emma's bassinet. "Are your bags packed, little Emma?" he asked, gently touching the velvety-soft cheeks.

The baby kicked her legs, encased in a knitted one-piece suit.

John chuckled softly. "That's my girl."

Lucy remained seated on the edge of her bed. "I could find some place to rent until Harry comes. I really don't want to impose."

"I told you it's no imposition. Now, you grab Emma, I'll grab your bags and we'll be on our way."

"We don't have a lot of luggage."

"Not to worry. Mom's been buying Emma a few things. You'll need a moving truck the next time you decide to move."

"What? What are you talking about?"

"Mom felt you needed more things. Don't worry about it. She loved doing the shopping."

"But I don't think I have enough money right now. I'll—I'll pay her back as soon as I get a job, but—"

"Lucy, you're part of the family. Don't forget that."

"That doesn't mean a lot to me. In our family—"

He stopped her with a finger to her lips, soft and supple beneath his touch. "You're in a different family now. In the Randall family."

Before Lucy could reply to that, Caroline stepped into the room. "Are you ready to go, Lucy?"

John noticed her hesitation. She refused to look at him when she said, "I'm not sure I should go with John. His mother has bought a lot of things for Emma. I can't pay her back."

"You don't understand, Lucy," Caroline said. "Camille doesn't expect you to pay her back. She just wants to make you as comfortable as she can."

"But, Dr. Randall, I'm not sure—"

"I'm sure," John said, no longer willing to listen to her beat herself up over the nonissue. Without awaiting her consent, he gathered up the bags. "I can probably handle Emma, too, if you'd like."

"No, I'll carry Emma," Lucy said, finally standing and moving to her daughter's bassinet. She lifted Emma out, wrapping her in a blanket. "Do you think she'll be warm enough, Dr. Randall?"

"I'm sure she will. John will turn on the heater in his truck, too, just to be sure. Right, John?"

"Right, Caro. We'd better go while the truck is still warm, Lucy." He started out the door.

Lucy stood there, holding her baby, not moving.

Noticing the hesitation, Caroline helped John's cause. She stepped toward Lucy and put an arm around her shoulders. "Lucy, Camille and John will take good care of the two of you, I promise."

With her voice shaking, Lucy said, "It's a little scary thinking about leaving here. I've been safe and happy here."

Caroline smiled. "It's pretty amazing to hear someone want to stay in the hospital. Most of our patients are anxious to leave."

"I'm just not sure—"

"I am. I know Camille and John very well. Neither one would harm a hair on your head, and certainly not Emma's."

John returned to the room. "What's taking so long? I've got the truck warming up and your bags in it. Now I can carry Emma and you can hold on to my arm, Lucy. Come along." He took Emma from her arms, gently pulling the blanket more closely across the baby, and waiting for Lucy to take his arm.

Caroline smiled at her. "You're on your way, Lucy. I'll check on you in a few days." She walked the couple to the door of the hospital and watched as John put Emma in the rear car seat, then helped Lucy into the truck.

He circled the truck and got behind the wheel.

"Are you sure her car seat is safe?" Lucy asked the moment he sat down.

"We bought the best kind available." He looked over his shoulder at Emma. "She looks fine."

"Yes, I guess so."

"Lucy, why are you feeling so unsettled?"

Lucy looked down at her tightly clenched hands. "I—I think it's because I'm leaving the hospital. I got comfortable there. Now I'm leaving it to go some place I haven't ever seen. It's difficult."

John reached over and put his hand over hers. "It will be all right, Lucy, I promise. If it's not, if you're unhappy, I'll take you wherever you want to go."

Her eyes grew larger. "Really? You'd do that?"

"I would, as long as you had some place to go. But

I think you'll find Mom a great hostess. She'll love you and your baby, just like a real grandmother."

"I don't understand why. I'm not sure my mother would even acknowledge my baby's birth if we lived next door. My father has a new family and doesn't even know I'm having a baby. Why would your mother care?"

"Because you're lovable, Lucy," John said slowly. "Your husband may not have noticed, because he was too wrapped up in his own feelings, or your parents, but I see a gentle, kind young woman who is going to make a wonderful mother."

His compliment elicited a blush that gave a glow to her cheeks. Her eyes looked down to her lap as she said, "Th-thank you, John."

Before he revealed too much of his sudden feelings for her, he changed approaches. "You know, in reality, you're going to be doing me and Dad a favor."

"I am?"

"Yeah, but you've got to promise not to tell Mom."

"Why? What are you talking about, John?"

"Mom had major surgery last year. Dad and I have been wanting her to slow down. We tried to get her to hire a housekeeper, but she refused. But with you there, maybe you can help her with some of her jobs taking care of the house. Not a lot. I know you've got Emma, but a little help would be nice. We'd just like to know that Mom is relaxing a little bit. Enjoying life more."

From the relaxed set of her shoulders John could see Lucy's tension evaporate. Her eyes nearly sparkled now when she spoke. "Of course! I'll be glad to help her. I've been wondering what I can do to repay her for all her kindness."

"Just remember, you can't tell Mom what you're doing. She'd be furious with us if she knew."

"Of course not, but I'll be glad to help out."

"Thanks, Lucy. That will make a difference in Mom's life. She can rock Emma some, too. She's been wanting a baby to cuddle for a long time."

Lucy turned to look at her sleeping baby. "Emma will be glad to volunteer for some cuddling. I think cuddling is a good thing."

"I think so, too," he said with a smile. And he knew just who he'd like to cuddle—the beautiful woman beside him.

After a few minutes John came to a stop outside his parents' house.

"This is nice, and quite large," Lucy said as she surveyed the ranch house.

"Yeah. That's why we think Mom needs some help." He knew his parents' house was large. And it was true that his father had tried to hire some help, but his mom had refused.

He came around the truck and opened the door. Then he reached up for Lucy, lifting her up and out of the seat. He held her gently, liking the feel of her in his arms.

"John… You can set me down now."

He realized then that he still held her. Slowly he set her on her feet, turned away and retrieved Emma. He gave the baby to her mother.

"Are your parents home?"

"Yeah. Mom should come running out at any moment." Even as he finished speaking, he saw the back door open and his mother emerge.

She ran excitedly to Lucy and hugged her and the baby. "I'm so glad you're here. Come in and see what I've set up for Emma. You may want to change it, but it'll give her a place to sleep peacefully right now."

Lucy went with Camille, as if she had a choice, but she seemed happy to go with his mother. John followed along behind, smiling at the picture the three of them made. He wanted to see Lucy when she discovered the room his mother had made up for her. And the small room next door, that had been a catchall for things for years, had been cleaned out and filled with a crib, a little chest and changing table for Emma.

Under his mother's instructions, he'd helped change the room into a small sanctuary for the baby.

Camille led the way to Lucy's bedroom, then stepped aside for Lucy to enter first.

"Oh, Mrs. Randall, it's beautiful. I never dreamed of anything like this."

"It's my daughter Melissa's old room. I'm glad to have it filled again. Now, come with me to Emma's little room."

She led Lucy next door to see the nursery.

"Oh, how darling! Emma will love it. And it's just next to mine so I will hear her easily."

"That's what I thought. Though I think I should get up with Emma the first few nights, so you can catch up on your sleep."

"Oh, no, I'm fine. I can manage."

"We'll see," Camille said.

"Or I could get up with her," John offered.

Both women turned to stare at him.

He raised both hands in surrender at their outraged expressions. "Okay, I'll leave it up to the two of you, unless you get too run-down and I happen to hear Emma."

His mother voiced her approval and Lucy nodded. John decided it was time to bring in the small amount of luggage Lucy had. "I'll be right back with your bags," he said.

When he got outside, he discovered his father walking up from the barn. "Any problems while I was gone?"

"Nope. I just thought I'd check on the mamas you had in the barn. Your mother was driving me crazy."

"I know. Lucy wasn't any calmer. As a matter of fact, I decided to tell Lucy we needed some help for Mom. It made her not feel so ungrateful. Gave her a way to pay Mom back. I hope that's okay."

"Sure, it's great, as long as your mother doesn't find out." They were almost to the back door when his father asked, "So Lucy is too proud to accept help?"

"No, I don't think it's that. She feels she's not worthy of all our attention. She's used to being ignored and unappreciated."

"Oh, yeah, that damn husband of hers. I'd almost forgotten about him."

"Believe me, Lucy hasn't."

"No, I'd guess not."

"Mike says he'll come after her."

"We'll be ready. I'll make sure there are some guns at hand, ready to be used."

"Yeah," John agreed as his father opened the door for him. He went through to Lucy's room and dropped off the larger of the two bags. Then he took the smaller one to Emma's room. The baby was already sleeping in the crib. John had to listen carefully to hear the gentle breathing of the baby. He reached out and patted her back, and she stirred. He continued to pat until she settled down again.

Then he stepped out of the baby's room just as Lucy came down the hall.

"Thank you, John, for bringing in our bags."

"Not a problem. Shouldn't you be lying down, resting?"

"That's what your mother said, but I tried to convince her I could do some cleaning. She wouldn't let me," Lucy said, frowning. "I'll try again later. I'll get her to let me help."

John smiled. "I'm sure you will, but you'd better take it easy the first few days, until you get your strength back."

"But I'm causing her more work, not less. If I don't help out, the strain on her might be too much!"

"She'll be okay for a few days. You go take a nap. I'll wake you up for dinner."

"Okay, but if I wake up earlier, I'll help prepare dinner. I can cook."

"I'm sure you can. Emma's asleep, so go get in bed."

He stood and watched as Lucy entered the bedroom Camille had made up for her. He wished he could follow her in and hold her in his arms. But he knew he couldn't, not when she was technically another man's wife. He waited until she'd gotten in bed to close the door so she wouldn't be disturbed…and he wouldn't be tempted.

Then he headed for the kitchen so he could have a talk with his mother.

His mother saw him coming and poured coffee in a mug for him as he joined his father at the breakfast table.

"I sent Lucy to take a nap," Camille told him.

"I know. Mom, you're going to need to let Lucy gradually do some work around here. It will make her feel she's contributing to her upkeep. Otherwise, she'll feel like she's a charity case."

"I know, dear, but not on the first day. She needs to get some rest."

"Yeah, she's gone to sleep, like little Emma."

His father leaned forward. "I was hoping to see the baby. I only saw her the day she was born."

"You will, Dad," John said. "She's already changed. She's started to look a lot like her mom now that she's recovered from being born."

"Well, I'm looking forward to seeing little Emma again."

"She's sleeping about three hours between bottles right now. Within the week, I think she'll last four hours between bottles. That will give Lucy plenty of time to rest." Camille looked perfectly satisfied with the situation.

"Don't overdo it, Cammy," Griff growled, using his pet name for his wife.

"Of course not! All I'm hoping is she'll let me rock the baby every once in a while." The sweet smile on Camille's face told her men how much she wanted to hold Emma.

LUCY GRADUALLY CAME AWAKE, thinking the nurses should be in soon. When she finally opened her eyes, she remembered that she no longer was in the hospital. John had brought her to his family's home early this afternoon.

She immediately got out of bed, in spite of her soreness, and hurried to Emma's little room next door. She panicked not to find her child in the crib. Immediately, she rushed to the family room.

Once there, she came to an abrupt halt. Camille sat in the rocking chair, Emma on her shoulder, as she talked the child into burping.

"Come now, little Emma, show Grandma what a good burper you are. Your Uncle John has been bragging on you."

As if she understood those words, Emma burped loudly, much to Camille's praise.

"She does that well, doesn't she?" Lucy said with a chuckle, startling Camille.

"Oh, I didn't realize you were there, Lucy," Camille said, smiling at her. "Emma and I were enjoying ourselves."

"It sounds like it. But you should've awakened me so I could take care of her. I don't want to add to your burdens."

"And I don't want to steal away your time with Emma. But I thought you could use a little extra sleep today. Moving is hard on us."

"Yes, I guess so. And I appreciate the care you're giving Emma."

"She is such a darling. Here, you take the rocker and visit with her a little. I've got a load of clothes I can bring in here and fold."

"I'll be glad to fold the clothes if you want—"

"No, no, I'll be glad to listen to you and Emma while I fold clothes. It'll be fun."

Camille gave up the rocker to Lucy and handed Emma down to her. "Now, I'll go get the clothes."

Lucy gathered her child to her, loving the soft, warm feel of her infant in her arms, inhaling her baby scent. "How are you, Emma? Do you like your new room? It's very pretty, isn't it?"

With Emma kicking her legs and waving her arms, Lucy imagined she was agreeing with her. "It was nice of Camille to feed you your bottle. Your appetite is growing, isn't it?"

Then she laid Emma down in her lap, so she could look at her face. "Did you behave yourself?"

Camille came in with a load of clothes as Lucy asked that question. "Of course she did. She was a darling."

"I'm glad. I've already discovered she has a little temper when she doesn't instantly get her bottle."

"All babies do. You should've heard John when he didn't get his bottle at once. He could raise the roof the first few months. Griff and I were so completely inexperienced, we'd run ourselves ragged to get the bottle to him as soon as he awakened. Then Mildred—she was Griff's family's housekeeper— was over here one day and told us crying was good for him. Let him cry a little."

"Really?" Lucy asked, her eyes wide.

"Really. After a little while, he stopped crying so vehemently. He knew we would come when we could." Camille had a smile on her lips as she reminisced.

Lucy thought John had certainly improved over the years. She thought of how he'd cared for her and Emma, how he'd looked after her that night in the truck. At the memory, shivers coursed through her body.

Why was she thinking of John that way?

To overcome those feelings, she asked, "How about Melissa?"

"Oh, she was terribly spoiled. If Griff or I didn't get there in time, John would be beside her bed, patting her, telling her we were coming."

"I've seen him pat Emma, too, telling her to be patient. How funny that he cautions patience in others when he was very demanding," Lucy said with a smile.

"I know. But he's such a caring soul. He always wants to make those around him feel okay."

"Yes, he does," Lucy said with a frown, remembering his care of her again, "even if they aren't his responsibility."

"But, Lucy, in John's mind you are his responsibility. After all, he's the one who found you when you were stranded on the road. He's the one who got you to the hospital and he's the one who discovered you are Harry's sister. He's going to be your brother until Harry comes back and can do that job."

She didn't want to think of John as a brother. That wasn't the feeling he evoked in her. But she didn't want to reveal that to John's mother. "I don't want him to be responsible for me. If I've learned anything, it's that I'm responsible for me. I blamed my marriage on my mother. But I'm the one who made that decision. Not her. I'm in charge of my life from now on."

"I'm glad to hear it."

At the sound of John's voice she started. Looking up, she saw him at the entrance to the family room. He looked so handsome, so strong, so male... She swallowed the desire to fly into his arms.

She breathed deeply before she spoke. "I was telling your mother that because she said you felt responsible for me. But you're not."

"Nope. I'm just trying to help out where I can. Besides, I'm Emma's Uncle John. She should get to know me while she can," he teased, leaning down to stroke Emma's cheek.

Emma turned her head in his direction, though her eyes didn't quite register where he was.

"That's my girl," he whispered.

The nearness of John, the smell of his aftershave, the whisper of his breath on her face was all too much for Lucy.

She had to get away from John before she embarrassed herself and kissed him—right in front of his mother.

She jumped up from the rocker, putting Emma on her shoulder. "I'm going to go put Emma down so I can help you get dinner on the table."

She was out of the room before either adult could protest.

"Did you upset Lucy?" Camille asked, frowning.

"Not intentionally. I'll go ask her."

John reached the door to Emma's room, finding Lucy bending over her daughter's crib.

"Lucy? Are you all right?"

She kept her face averted. "Yes, of course. I'm just putting Emma to bed."

"Need any help?"

"No, of course not." She wanted him to come to her without a reason. "She just takes a little time to settle."

By the time she'd finished speaking, she discovered John at her elbow. "She's staying awake a little bit more, isn't she?" she asked.

"She's only three days old."

"I know, but she's already changed a lot." Hard to believe that she'd only known John for four days. It seemed so much longer. He seemed so important to her…and to Emma.

"Yeah."

"I think she's asleep now," Lucy said, backing away from the crib.

"Okay. Are you going to help Mom put dinner on the table?"

"Yes, I thought I would."

"Okay. I've got to go back to the barn, but I'll be back in time for dinner. I'm starving."

She couldn't prevent a response to his remark. "It seems to me I've heard you say that before, John," she said with a chuckle.

"You're right. It seems to be a normal state for me."

As for her own state, she thought, it would be arousal.

Chapter Five

They were sitting down to eat when John heard a sound he was beginning to recognize. He excused himself and hurried to the nursery. There he found Emma, staring up at the animal mobile hanging over her crib.

"Hello, little Emma. Did you have a good nap?"

Since he didn't expect an answer, he reached out and picked up the baby, putting her on his shoulder. He walked back to the kitchen with Emma kicking and waving her arms.

"Hey, there, look who's up for dinner," he said, swinging Emma down into his arms. "See, Dad? She's as beautiful as ever."

"Yes, you're right, son," Griff said, reaching out for the baby. "I think it's time for me to hold her again."

"I'll fix her bottle, Mr. Randall. Then I can take her, if you're tired of holding her." Lucy jumped up from the table and began fixing a bottle.

"I'd like to feed her just this once, Lucy, if you don't mind."

"No, of course not, if—if you really want to," Lucy managed to say.

"Oh, I really do. I love feeding a baby. They are so perfect at this age, aren't they?"

"Yes, of course."

John laughed. "And I thought I'd get to feed her since I'm the one who heard her cry."

"Age before beauty, son, except that applies to Lucy instead of you. And you're right. Emma looks like her mama."

Lucy's cheeks turned bright red. "Thank you, Mr. Randall."

"Let's make it Griff, honey. There are too many Mr. Randalls in Rawhide."

"Yes, sir."

Griff looked at his wife. "Is she going to be this formal all the time?"

"No, dear. Just give her time to settle in," Camille said with a smile toward Lucy.

"Here's the bottle…Griff," Lucy said with a reluctant smile.

"Good girl, Lucy. Now, watch an expert feed the baby!"

Lucy did exactly that. She sat down next to Griff and carefully watched him feed her child.

"Hey! I can do it as well as you, Dad." John leaned in and smiled at Emma.

"She's not going to pay any attention to you when I've got the bottle, son."

"Next time I hear her cry, I'll capture the bottle first and then go get the baby. Then she'll stay with me." John's good-natured grin showed he was teasing.

"And if I'd known Emma would be this popular, I would've come here immediately after giving birth!" Lucy said, which brought laughs from the other three.

"I could've told you we'd be fighting over her. We haven't had a baby around here in close to thirty years," Camille said.

"Babies are special, aren't they?" Lucy said with a soft smile.

"Just remember you said that when this little darling wants a bottle in the middle of the night," Griff said.

"I don't mind."

"I suspect you'll have volunteers then, too," John said.

"Oh, no, I'm going to get up quickly so she doesn't disturb your sleep. She's already getting a little spoiled because she gets so much attention."

John grinned even more. "That's not going to change, Lucy."

"Some people don't like babies," Lucy said hesitantly.

"That's true, Lucy, but you won't find any of them in this family," Griff said. "And if you're talking about that husband of yours, don't even think about him. He's all messed up. Just keep little Emma away from him."

"Yes. I don't intend for him to know that Emma survived. Caroline said he was trying to provoke a miscarriage."

John shook his head. "That's disgusting."

"I—I'm so grateful to all of you for your caring and concern for Emma. She's a lucky little girl."

John gave her a sharp look. "And we're going to keep her…and you—that way."

Griff put Emma on his shoulder and helped her perform her incredible burping that brought laughter even from her mother.

"Yep, you're a mighty talented young lady," Griff assured the infant, giving her a small kiss on her cheek. He looked at his son. "Now, don't tell me you can get that good a burp from her."

"I sure can. That's one of her particular talents."

The ringing phone interrupted their laughter. Camille got up to answer it. "Oh, how nice. Just a minute and I'll ask her." She covered the receiver. "Lucy, the ladies at the ranch wondered if you and me and Emma would like to come to lunch tomorrow."

"Do you think Emma is old enough to go out?" Lucy asked anxiously.

"Of course she is. It's better to go when all the children are in school and the men are out working. Then it will just be us ladies who want to hold her."

"Poor little girl's going to come home exhausted," Griff said with a smile.

"Will it make her too tired?" Lucy asked.

"Yes, but it won't hurt her any. It just means she might sleep a little longer tomorrow."

"Oh, that's all right. But what does Camille mean by the ladies at the ranch?"

"She's referring to the main Randall ranch, where my cousins live. There are four ladies married to the original Randalls and several of the next generation of Randalls, too," Griff explained.

Camille returned to the phone and made arrangements.

When she got off the phone, Lucy said, "It's very nice of all of them to invite us over."

Camille smiled. "Yes, it is, isn't it? It's been a couple of years since they've had a brand-new baby there, too."

"It's probably time for Jim and Patience to have another one," Griff said. "Their little girl is two, isn't she?"

"I think so," Camille said. "She's the cutest little thing."

"She'll be there tomorrow?" Lucy asked.

"Oh, yes, along with Patience and Jim's sister, Elizabeth, too. They wanted to come see you at the hospital, but Caroline said she thought you needed your rest."

"I had no idea anyone wanted to visit me."

"That's okay, Lucy," John assured her. "You'll get them sorted out tomorrow."

"I've never known such a large family," she muttered.

"I'm sure there are other large families," Griff said, "but what makes this family special is that we all get along and help each other."

"Yes, that is special. My family is small, but we don't get along."

"Harry is a really nice guy," John said.

"Yes. And you'll notice he didn't hang around his family," Lucy pointed out.

"She's got a point there, son," Griff said.

"Oh, look. Emma's gone to sleep. I'll go put her in her bed," Lucy said, getting up at once.

She gently lifted the little girl from Griff's arms, thanking him for feeding her, and hurried out of the kitchen.

"She's a cute little thing, isn't she?" Griff asked to no one in particular.

"I told you she's a beautiful baby," John said.

"I wasn't talking about Emma," Griff said, looking at his son.

"Oh, you mean Lucy. Yeah, I told you the baby looked like her mother. But Lucy doesn't think so."

"And she and Harry come from the same family?"

Camille nodded. "Yes, some women treat their daughters different from their sons."

"I think we should claim Lucy and Emma for our family. They deserve to be Randalls," Griff said.

John said, "They've got my vote. I don't think Harry will object, either."

"I doubt that Harry has any idea of the life Lucy has led. He was six years older than her. He left home to go to college when she was twelve. He probably doesn't know her very well."

"That still seems weird, Mom. I mean, didn't he go back home for holidays and summers?"

"I doubt it. He probably worked while he went to school. I don't believe he was on scholarship."

"I forgot that some families aren't as fortunate we are."

"True, son," Griff said. "Not everyone has a trust fund."

"Or a dad who's an expert investor to keep it growing." John grinned at his father.

"Thank you. I'll take those words to heart, son. We'll—" He broke off as Lucy came back in. "Did she stay asleep?"

"Yes, Griff, she did. You did a very good job."

"Good. It was a pleasure, Lucy."

"You are all so good about Emma. I can't tell you how much I appreciate it, but you don't have to pretend. Babies can be difficult, and I'll understand if you get irritated by her crying…or anything."

John and Camille started to protest, but Griff held up his hand. "Lucy, we love babies, all babies. Emma won't wear us out, and we're delighted to help you with her."

"Thank you," Lucy said. But her eyes filled with tears. A second later she turned and ran from the room.

JOHN PULLED HIS HORSE to a halt and shoved back his sleeve to check the time. It was two o'clock. The ladies should be back from the luncheon. He pulled out his cell phone and dialed the number at the house.

Listening to the unanswered rings, he frowned. Why weren't they back? Emma needed to sleep in her own crib, and Lucy would be exhausted. After all, she had a baby less than a week ago. His mother should know better than to keep them out so long.

"Hey, John!" one of his cowboys called, drawing his attention. He supposed he should pay attention to what was going on, but he had trouble keeping his mind on cows lately. He was worried about Emma and Lucy.

Fifteen minutes later, he called the house again. Still no answer. He waited another fifteen minutes before he called his mother's cell phone. When she answered, his first question was, "Why haven't you brought Lucy and Emma home, Mom? They need their rest."

"Hello, to you, too, John."

"Sorry, Mom, but I'm worried about Emma and Lucy."

"Emma is sleeping peacefully. Lucy is a little tired, but I'm putting her to bed as soon as we get home."

"When will that be?"

"Probably by three, or maybe three-thirty."

"I hope she doesn't overdo it. She'll have a hard time if she does."

"Quit fussing, John. I'll get her in bed as soon as we get home, I promise."

He could hear laughter in his mother's voice. "I'm not being difficult, Mom. I'm just worried about them."

"I know. We'll be on our way in a few minutes."

"Good to hear."

He put his phone away and went back to herding cows. But his mind was on Lucy and Emma. And he was wishing he was at home to wait for them.

Hoping to get in earlier than he'd planned, John pushed the herd a little harder. He could help Lucy with Emma if she needed it. And she would if she didn't get enough sleep.

At best, she'd only get a couple of hours to nap before it was time to get up for supper. She'd have trouble getting up with Emma later in the night. Maybe he'd stay up a little later to feed Emma her first bottle around midnight.

He could manage staying up that late. He could even set his alarm. Get a couple of hours of sleep and then get up with Emma.

An unruly cow grabbed his attention and he decided he'd better concentrate on the job at hand. He wouldn't be able to help anyone if he fell out of the saddle.

"OH, THERE YOU ARE, JOHN," Camille said as she heard her son come in. "We thought we'd have to eat dinner without you."

"Sorry." So much for his plan to come in early. Now he was even later than usual. "One of the boys got thrown from his horse because of a snake," he explained.

"Was he hurt?" Griff asked. "And who was it?"

"Jerry. He's got a new girl and wasn't concentrating on his job." John hoped his cheeks weren't as red as he feared they were. He knew exactly how Jerry felt. It could easily have been him thrown from his horse for all the focus he had today.

"Was he hurt badly?" Camille asked.

"No, he just sprained an ankle when he landed on it. He'll stay in tomorrow and probably be all right after that." He turned to see Lucy sitting at the table.

"Hey, Lucy, how are you doing?"

"Feeling lazy. Your mom insisted I take a nap and she didn't wake me up until a few minutes ago. She even fed Emma her bottle and put her back to bed. I never heard her cry."

"Good for Mom. I was afraid you would be exhausted by your outing."

"No, Camille made sure I wasn't. And we had such a good time. I got to know all of them, especially Patience. They were so nice to me."

"Good. They're all great ladies."

Lucy nodded. "Patience told me how her husband, Jim, saved her from her son's father. What a story!"

"And you think your story is dull?" John asked.

Lucy blushed. The color looked good on her, he thought. "Well, the man sounded crazy…and mean."

"He was both of those things," Griff agreed. "And if the sheriff hadn't shot him, he might've caused Jim and Patience a lot of trouble."

"Mike seems so nice, though," Lucy said.

"It wasn't Mike. It was his uncle. He's retired now. Mike became sheriff when his uncle retired the first time. Then he came back and Mike was going to go back to Chicago, and Caroline talked her father into finding a way for Mike to stay." Camille smiled at Lucy. "She already knew she was in love with him."

"Jake also thought Mike was the better lawman," Griff added. "It wasn't just Caro's feelings that had Jake looking for a way to keep Mike here."

"Of course, dear, you're right," Camille agreed. "But it worked out well for Caro, also."

"True," Griff agreed.

"All the stories they told at lunch were so wonderful!" Lucy exclaimed. "Even Jake and B.J.'s story was interesting."

"I don't think I've heard that one," John said. "As

a matter of fact, I only know the stories of this generation."

"Oh, you should hear your parents' story. It was very good, too. Especially when they included your grandfather."

John sat up straighter. "Granddad? What about him?"

Griff and Camille suddenly seemed engrossed in their dinner. Looking at them, Lucy tried to cover. "I—I'm not sure. I may have the story wrong."

John stared at her for several seconds before he turned to his parents. "Why is she backing up? What's going on here?"

Griff looked at his wife. "Camille, I can't believe you told Lucy that story."

"I didn't! Some of the girls got carried away and told it before I could remember to stop them."

John glared at his parents. "I don't think it's fair for Lucy to know the story when I don't."

"I think it's time for dessert," Camille announced.

"I'll help you clean up before you serve," Lucy said, getting up, grateful for the interruption.

"No, Lucy, you need to rest. I'll help her serve." Without pausing, John got up and began clearing the table.

"Does that mean he's forgotten?" Lucy whispered to Griff when the others had left the table.

"I don't think so," Griff replied.

"What can we do?"

"You could stop whispering behind my back," John pointed out from behind them.

Lucy flushed bright red.

"And, no, I haven't forgotten. We'll continue the discussion during dessert." John cleared a platter, not saying anything else.

Lucy stared at Griff. "What do I do?" she mouthed.

"Nothing. It will be all right," Griff mouthed back.

Camille carried a chocolate cake to the table. "I made Red's chocolate cake for dessert."

"Why is this Red's chocolate cake?" Lucy asked.

"Oh, it's a special recipe that Red kept to himself for many years. He only decided to give it out last year." Lucy had met Red earlier that day at the ranch. The older cowboy had made such an impression on her that she wasn't surprised how much he meant to all the Randalls.

"Nice try, girls," John said as he sat down. "But I'm not distracted. Okay, Dad. Tell the story of how you and Mom met and what Granddad had to do with it."

Griff took a bite of chocolate cake and chewed it. Then he looked at John. "I thought we'd told you about me finding my family. Camille was staying with Megan for a few days and that's how we met."

"Yeah, and what did Granddad have to do with it?"

"Not much."

John looked at Lucy, who was keeping her gaze on her cake.

"I don't think that's really fair, Griff," Camille said. She looked at her son. "Your father didn't know who his father was because his mother had never told him. She had lied to him about…things."

"What things? I don't remember you mentioning my grandmother," John said, turning to stare at his father.

"My mother had an affair and ran away pregnant at seventeen," Griff said. He squared his jaw. "She told me a lot of lies and taught me to hate the man who fathered me. I came here to bury her, as she requested. That's how I found my family. And they wouldn't let me go. You know how Jake is. Well, I look a lot like them. He kept insisting I stay. And then there was Camille."

"But how does Granddad figure in?"

"He'd tried to get in touch with Griff's mother, but she refused to let him see his son. When he heard that Griff was here, he came to Jake and asked him if he could tell Griff. Jake said he would when the time was right. But Granddad couldn't wait. He showed up at an…inconvenient time and insisted on being introduced."

John turned to his father. "That must've been awkward."

"Yeah."

"That's all you've got to say?" John asked.

"We worked things out. By the time you came along, Granddad was part of the family."

"And he left you his ranch."

"Yeah."

"So why didn't you tell me earlier?"

"I didn't want to embarrass your grandfather. He was ashamed of having had an affair with a seventeen-year-old. Why should I make him feel ashamed all over again?"

"I suppose you're right," John said, slowly eating his cake.

Lucy sent a hesitant smile to him. "It's a wonderful family, John."

"Yeah."

"You're lucky to be a part of it."

"Now you're part of it, too, Lucy."

"Not really. But thank you for the thought."

Chapter Six

That night, Lucy heard her baby cry and she struggled out of bed. She couldn't let Emma cry—and she might wake up the rest of the family.

No! Lucy admonished herself. They weren't part of the family. She and Emma were on their own. Or at least they would be on their own. She hurried on to get her child, even though she'd stopped her wailing. When she reached Emma's little room, she came to an abrupt stop at the sight before her.

There stood John with Emma in his arms.

"What are you doing?" she demanded.

"I'm going to get Emma's bottle. Go back to bed."

"But, John, you have to get up early in the morning. Here, give me Emma. I'll go fix her bottle."

"Nope. I'm feeding Emma right now. You can get up at four when she'll be up again."

"No! I'm not supposed to make your life harder by coming here. I'll take Emma and go away if it's going to make things more difficult."

John bent down and kissed Lucy's cheek. "Go to bed now, Lucy, or I'll wake up Mom and she can tell you."

"No, you can't do that!"

"Then go to bed and get up at four. Emma will wake you up."

She stifled a yawn. "Okay, but just this once."

"Sure."

JOHN CUDDLED EMMA against his chest as he fixed her bottle. "You know, sweetheart, feeding you during the night isn't so bad a job, even if I do miss some sleep."

He screwed the nipple on her bottle and moved into the den to settle in the rocking chair. "Okay, little girl, here you go."

He watched her suck down her milk as he slowly rocked back and forth. She was so little, though he thought she'd already grown since her birth. It didn't take her long to finish. John eased her up on his shoulder and rubbed her back until she burped.

Then he gently patted her back until he could hear her breathing deepening and he knew she was asleep. He got up from the rocker and carried her back to her crib, where he covered her with her blanket.

As tired as he was, he stood there, smiling down at the baby, thinking how beautiful she was. A true miracle.

He'd always thought he'd have kids of his own by now. He'd figured he'd have married young. Why not? He had a good job, he could take care of a wife and family, even build a new house for a future wife. He'd dated more than his share of local girls, even considered asking one of them to marry him. But in the end, he couldn't quite bring himself to commit, not when he'd yet to find the kind of love his parents shared.

Strange that he was struck by love on a dark night more than an hour out of town by a pregnant married woman.

It wasn't a good situation. But somehow it didn't matter. Lucy had needed him then. He still remembered those hours in the truck holding her in his arms. Arms that ached to hold her again…and again.

But he couldn't. Not yet.

Instead he held Emma, so her mommy could sleep. He hoped Lucy knew he did that for her, because as much as he loved Emma, he loved her mother more.

THE NEXT MORNING, after Lucy had fed her baby and played with her, Lucy put her in her crib and went to the kitchen.

"May I have a cup of coffee?" Lucy asked.

"Of course, dear. The pot's always on."

"I wanted to apologize for bringing up the story about how you and Griff met. I didn't realize John wouldn't know."

"I had forgotten he and Melissa didn't know. We didn't think we should tell them because of their grandfather. He was greatly embarrassed by his past."

"I can imagine. I'm glad John took it as well as he did."

"Yes. He's a good boy. I shouldn't say that. He's a man now, not a boy."

"Yes, he is. He got up with Emma at midnight. I tried to get him to go back to bed, but he threatened to wake you up."

Camille laughed. "He's a little hardheaded."

"I realized that. I finally went to sleep, but I felt badly, knowing he'd be up at six."

"He was worried about you getting too tired from our luncheon yesterday. He's such a worrywart."

"That was thoughtful of him." More than thoughtful. It was so caring of John. He was willing to suffer himself if it would help her.

"Yes, it was."

"Well, I'd better go put some clothes into the wash. I'm afraid I'm going to wear out your washer and dryer with all the washing for Emma."

"Babies are like that. And it will be that way for at least two years."

"I'll have to find a place to lease with a good washer and dryer."

Camille stared at Lucy. Then she picked up Lucy's coffee cup and moved into the kitchen. "Yes, of course."

Camille warned herself she couldn't hold Lucy against her will. She could leave if that was her choice. But Camille realized how much she wanted Lucy and Emma to stay. She'd just have to work on Harry and Melissa when they came back.

WHEN JOHN CAME IN just before dark, Lucy was in the kitchen, helping his mother get dinner ready.

"Did you take a nap today?" he asked without saying hello.

Camille looked at her son. "Why no, dear, I didn't. But then, I wasn't tired."

"Mom, you know I'm talking to Lucy."

"Oh, I'm sorry. I didn't realize that. Did you, Lucy?"

"No, I didn't." Lucy kept her head down, filling a bowl with black-eyed peas.

"Excuse me. Lucy, did you take a nap today?"

She set the pan in the sink and filled it with water before she looked at him. "No, I didn't. I wasn't tired."

"You can't expect to get up all night with Emma if you don't get enough sleep."

"I don't think I did get up with Emma every time last night…did I?" Lucy arched an eyebrow.

"What do you mean?" Griff eyed the two of them.

John turned bright red and looked at his parents. "I—I got up with Emma at midnight."

"But, dear, if you're getting up at six in the morning, how can you possibly get up at midnight with Emma?" Camille asked.

"One time didn't hurt, Mom. After you went to that luncheon, you knew Lucy would be tired. She needed more rest than she was going to get from a nap."

Griff put a hand on both Camille's and John's shoulders. "We can discuss this later. Right now I think dinner is ready."

"Oh, yes, of course," Camille said.

John turned to stare at his father. "I don't think this is something we need to discuss. I was just trying to help Lucy."

"I know, son. But your mother has a point. You need sleep. Accidents have happened before, you know."

His father pulled him to his place. "Sit down, son. You don't want to have this argument now."

"What argument? I'm just trying to—"

"We're ready to eat now." Camille sat down at the table and looked at John and her husband. "Aren't you going to join us, you two?"

"Yeah," John growled, shifting to dislodge his father's hold.

Lucy stared at first John and then Griff. Quietly, she said, "If I'm causing problems in your family, I can leave."

Griff grinned at her. "No, you're not causing problems. Besides, we always have problems. You should've lived here with my daughter before she went to France."

Lucy looked at Griff, a question in her eyes. "She went to France? For a trip, you mean?"

"Oh, no. Her mother insisted I let her go to France for a semester. And it took her six years to come home."

"My, that's a long trip."

"Melissa designs jewelry and she started working for a well-known designer in France," Camille explained. "She didn't come back until I needed surgery."

"And that's when Harry met her?"

"Yeah," John said. "And he never had a chance. One look at her and it was all over." Just as it was with him, he thought, after one look at Lucy. Strange that both he and Harry fell for the other's sister.

"She must be really beautiful."

"Yes, she is," Camille said with a big smile. "She looks like her father."

"No, sweetheart, she takes after you," Griff said with a smile. "The only difference is that her hair is dark, like mine."

"That's nice, but can someone pass the meat, please," John said, interrupting.

Lucy picked up the platter of chicken-fried steak and passed it across the table to John. "Are you hungry, John?"

"I'm starved."

"He's always hungry when he gets in in the evening," Camille told her.

"Does he get grumpy if he doesn't get food right away, like Emma?" Lucy asked with a smile.

"Exactly," Camille agreed.

"So have some peas, John," Lucy said, passing the bowl. "And mashed potatoes."

John filled his plate high, then grunted as he shoveled in food.

Several minutes later, John realized Lucy was staring at him. "What's wrong?"

"Where do you put all of that?"

"All of what?"

"The food."

John shrugged. "I get hungry when I ride all day. A cowboy has a voracious appetite."

He had a voracious appetite, all right. For her.

Swallowing the thought, he averted his eyes from her beautiful face. Just before Lucy got up and ran from the room.

Lucy buried her face in her arms and let the tears escape.

She knew she was hormonal after just having had her baby, but even she was surprised by how many tears she shed. And all because she was in lo— No, she refused to say the word. She tried again. All because she had feelings for John. Feelings she had no right to at this point in her life.

"Lucy?"

Hearing his voice at her closed door, she covered her head even more. "Go away!" she choked out.

"I can't do that. I want to know why you're crying."

"No!"

He didn't say anything and Lucy wasn't going to look to see if he'd gone.

"Come back and eat your dinner."

"No, I'm not hungry."

"Lucy, you've scarcely eaten. Come finish your dinner."

"No, I—I can't."

She heard him open the door, felt him sit down on the edge of her bed. Then his hand settled on her shoulder and pulled her back so he could look at her face. "What's going on?"

"N-nothing," she said, trying to avoid looking him in the eye.

"Why are you crying?"

"It—it just happens when you have a baby."

"If that's true, why are you hiding? Why not come back to dinner?"

She let her head drop. Then she nodded. "Yes, of course, I'm coming back to the table." She was a mature adult, after all, capable of being courteous and cordial despite her breaking heart.

"Good. You need to eat a good meal."

"I need to wash my face. Then I'll come back to the table."

John paused and Lucy held her breath. "Okay, I'll go on ahead. But you'll come?"

"Yes, I'll come." And she'd stare her feelings right in the eye, dare them to overcome her.

She didn't go to the bathroom until after he'd left her room. Then she went in and washed her face. She was horribly embarrassed. Now she had to go to the table and face the Randalls.

And hope she could avoid a detailed questioning.

JOHN WENT BACK to the table. "Lucy will be here in a minute. I think we shouldn't ask too many questions."

"But why was she crying?"

"I'm not sure, Mom. We need to give her some space."

"You think so?" Griff asked. "She won't maybe think about leaving?"

John frowned. "I don't think so."

About that time they heard Lucy coming down the hall. She slipped into her chair and muttered an apology. With her head down, she ate a decent meal. John knew because he kept an eye on her.

Just as they finished, she asked, "Is my car parked at Larry's garage?"

"Why, yes, it's there," John said. "Did you need it?"

"I just wondered."

John looked at his father. Could his dad be right? Was Lucy planning on leaving? But he wasn't sure why she was upset. She'd put him off by saying it was because she'd just given birth. But there was no way he was letting her leave.

Lucy went to the kitchen with his mother to help with the cleanup. But she didn't look anyone in the eye. Which meant she was doing exactly as she'd planned from the time he forced her out of her bedroom.

She was going away.

With Emma.

Not if he could help it. She wouldn't last long trying to hide from Cecil and provide for her baby.

He couldn't keep his promise and protect her from Cecil if she lived somewhere else. So why was she running away? What did she have to hide?

Lucy had no choice but to hide her feelings. And run. That had become clear to her as she'd sat across from John at dinner. She'd been so aware of him, so attracted to him, she could barely swallow. Staying here near John was no longer possible.

After she'd run from dinner, she'd spent the rest of the night trying to figure out the fastest way to reach her car. But all she came up with was to walk to Rawhide. It took a fifteen-minute car ride. How long would it take her to walk it, carrying Emma?

She couldn't take much. Lying in bed in the dark, she carefully thought out what she could take. In the closet was a backpack she'd seen when she'd arrived. She planned only a change of clothes for her, but Emma would need more. If she packed tightly, she thought she could fit enough of the baby's clothing.

Without a washer and dryer, she'd need a lot. Maybe she could manage to make it until she found a motel with laundry facilities.

And of course she'd need food, too. It made Lucy wish she were nursing her child. But because she'd been afraid she might not survive, she wanted her child to be bottle-fed.

She'd also have to take breakfast for herself. She wouldn't be able to stop anywhere in Rawhide or nearby. John might come looking for her, so she couldn't leave clues.

Not even if she wanted to.

Leaving John was something she tried not to think about. He'd said he would keep her safe, but he wouldn't want to when he discovered she loved him. That was why she had to leave.

She heard Emma starting to wake up. Her child didn't start crying at once. She would squirm around and make sweet sounds. Lucy had learned to recognize those sounds. She got out of bed and hurried to the crib.

"Hello, sweet angel. I know you're awake and want your bottle, but we need to get you all dry first. See, here's a dry diaper. They make you feel good, don't they?"

After she fastened the diaper, she pulled Emma's nightgown down. "Now you're ready for your bottle. Let's go fix it so you can drink it down. Then we'll have to go."

She kept telling herself they were doing the right thing. But she didn't believe it. She didn't want to leave. John was wonderful and he'd promised to protect her. But she couldn't ask that of him. He shouldn't risk his life for someone who didn't, couldn't, give back to him.

But she must not confess that to John.

She fixed Emma's bottle and sat in the rocker—for the last time—to feed her. Emma gladly sucked on the bottle, not realizing she'd soon be leaving this comfortable home.

After burping Emma, she rose and put the baby back in her crib. Then she went to her own room and got the backpack out of the closet. She packed one change of clothes for herself in the bottom of the pack. Then she went to Emma's room and hurriedly picked out as many pieces of baby clothing as she could get in the bag with room left at the top for the powdered food that she could mix with water to make bottles.

After that, she went to the kitchen and made up another bottle to have ready when Emma woke up three or four hours later.

Packing it, she shrugged the backpack on one shoulder and headed for Emma's room. She gently picked up her baby and wrapped her in a blanket, then covered her with another, heavier one.

Taking a deep breath, she said goodbye to the Randalls and tiptoed to the back door.

Till a deep voice, one that she recognized, said, "Going somewhere?"

Chapter Seven

Lucy almost dropped her most precious bundle, she was so startled.

She clutched the baby tightly. "Wh-what are you doing out here?"

"Waiting for you. Where are you going?"

Sighing, she mustered her courage and faced him. "John, I have to go. Will you give me a ride to Rawhide so I can get my car?"

"Why?"

"Because I need it. How else will I get away?"

"Why are you leaving?"

Lucy swallowed hard. "I—I don't want you to suffer. It's better if I go away."

"And does Emma deserve that?"

"I'll take care of Emma."

"And if your husband finds you?"

"As long as I keep moving, he won't find me." At least she prayed that was true.

John reached out for Emma. "Give her to me before you squeeze all the air out of her."

"No, I—" Conceding, she let John take her baby.

"How are you, little Emma? Was Mommy squeezing you?"

"No!" Lucy answered in place of Emma. "I—I'll take care of her."

He started back into the house. "Come in to the kitchen. Let's have a cup of coffee."

"I need to leave, John. I—I have to reach my car before dawn."

"Sit down," he ordered, and began putting on coffee with one hand, holding Emma with the other.

Realizing she wasn't going to convince him without talking things over, she took over the coffee-making duties.

John moved to a chair and held Emma in his arms, talking to the sleeping baby.

She couldn't help listening.

"Your mama thinks she's doing the best she can for you, but she's wrong. I don't know why she's doing this. She won't give me a reason, but she can't have a good enough reason to put you at risk."

Her hands jerked and she spilled coffee. Wiping up the mess, she said nothing.

John continued, "She needs to understand that nothing she feels would make this move worthwhile. Whether she tells me the reason or not."

Lucy sat down at the table knowing she had no choice now but to tell him the truth. Taking a deep breath she said, "I don't think you and your parents realize how difficult Cecil is. He wouldn't hesitate to kill you if you stood in his way."

"I figured that out." John smiled gently at Lucy.

"But I also know Emma is doing fine. And you've suffered enough, Lucy."

Tears filled her eyes and she blinked them back. "I don't know if I ever loved him. But whatever I'd felt for him had disappeared shortly after we married. I tried to remain true to my marriage vows, but it was all over after he beat me and tried to hurt Emma. But that doesn't mean I should use you to deal with Cecil."

John reached out and his palm caressed her cheek. "You did the best you could, and you have nothing to hang your head about."

"But you shouldn't— It's not your fault!"

Emma stirred, as if in response to the anguish of her mother's voice.

John patted Emma's back and soothed her with his deep voice. As always, she responded and settled back down.

"Please, John," Lucy begged in a whisper, "it's not your fault. I can't thank you enough."

"Okay, I'll let you have a pass this time, I promise. But you have to promise not to run away again. We don't want to protect only Emma. We want to protect you, too, Lucy."

"I don't deserve your protection, John. *I* married Cecil. *I* didn't leave when he first hit me. I thought he'd stop. He promised he would…."

"Honey, it doesn't matter what you did. You didn't deserve being hit. No one does. But you didn't have any support from your family. You didn't know about men like Cecil."

Lucy covered her face as tears began to fall. "I—I tried to be good but…it must've been me. I didn't—"

"Lucy, it's not your fault." John reached out with his free hand and pulled her into his lap, with Emma on his other shoulder. "It's all right, Lucy," he soothed. "It's all right."

For several minutes she let him cradle her, treat her with the kindness no man had shown her. Then finally John leaned forward and kissed her forehead.

"It's all right, Lucy. You're going to be a wonderful mom to Emma. I promise."

"John, you're so good to me." More tears wet her cheeks.

John smiled at her. "It's easy to be nice to you, Lucy. You're sweet and thoughtful and kind…" He leaned down and kissed her forehead again. "Your husband was so wrapped up in himself, he never even saw you." He wrapped his palm around her cheek, cradling her face, wiping her tears. He looked at her red-rimmed eyes and felt an overwhelming urge to kiss her, love her, protect her.

Lucy shook her head. "You don't understand. Cecil agreed with my mother. He thought I was ugly."

"Then he's a blind man." He lifted her face and caressed her cheek with his thumb. "You are the most beautiful woman I've ever met."

Lucy stirred against his hold, clearly uncomfortable with the compliments. "I—I should put Emma back in bed."

"I'll help you. Then I'll tuck you in, too. Remember, you promised not to run."

"I'll remember. John, thank you for making me feel better. I won't take Emma away without telling you. You've been a good friend to both of us."

He didn't want to be just her friend, but if that was all she offered, then he'd have to settle for it.

"Good. Let's go tuck Emma into her crib. I think she's missing it."

"Probably. She's lucky to have such a nice room."

"I think she deserves it," he said with a smile as he put his arm around Lucy and started them down the hall. Once they reached the nursery, he took Emma off his shoulder and laid her into her crib.

Lucy pulled the cover over her little girl and patted her back.

"She'll have you up in a couple of hours, so we'd better tuck you in, too."

"Will you get up and ride out tomorrow?" Lucy asked anxiously.

"No. My manager will be in charge tomorrow. I figured I'd lose sleep over you and Emma. And it's well worth it. So I'll be around tomorrow to help out with anything."

"You've already helped a lot."

"I'm here for you, Lucy. I promise."

They walked next door to her room, and Lucy turned to him. "Thank you again."

"Sleep in in the morning."

"No, I—"

He bent and kissed her lips, stopping her. "Sleep in. I'll be here when you wake up."

He left her room, pulling the door behind him.

Lucy stared after him, touching her lips. It was the first time he'd really kissed her. It wasn't a passionate kiss, rather a gentle one. Just like the man himself. Cecil hadn't indulged in that type of caress. In fact, he hadn't ever wasted time on any kind of caress.

From the time John first met her, he'd welcomed her into his arms for protection. She'd been charmed that first night. Now she couldn't deny she was in love with him.

God help her.

INSTEAD OF EATING BREAKFAST with his men in the bunkhouse at six, John got up at seven-thirty and wandered into the kitchen. "Good morning."

Camille stared at her son. "John! Don't you usually ride out? What's going on?"

"I stayed up last night to visit with Lucy when she packed up Emma and planned on walking to Rawhide to get her car. I thought it would be a good idea for us to talk. After a while, she promised not to run away again."

"But why would she do that?" Camille asked, anguish in her voice.

"She was afraid we wouldn't realize how dangerous her husband could be and he might hurt one of us when we've been so good to her."

"The poor dear. I've never been in that kind of situation. Who knows what I would do?"

"I know, Mom."

Beside her, Griff advised, "You need to tell her that, Cammy."

"Yes, I will. She needs to know how brave I think she is."

"I tried to tell her that, Mom. It's just that Lucy isn't used to being trusted and believed in."

"That poor child. She must've been in a terrible mess with that man hitting her. How could he?"

"We all wonder that, Mom." John did more than wonder. He vowed to protect Lucy. Even if he had to harm Cecil to do it.

LUCY GOT UP EVERY TIME Emma awakened. But she also went back to sleep. She didn't want to face John.

She hadn't been prepared for the kiss he'd given her last night.

In her marriage sex had been awful. A duty, an obligation, an act to please her husband. She didn't want anything to do with sex ever again. But with John, she wasn't so sure. When he held her, kissed her, something inside her came to life.

Desire.

And it frightened her to death.

When Emma woke her up at eight, Lucy knew she was going to have to face John. She changed Emma's diaper and dressed herself, too.

Then she headed for the kitchen, and John.

The three Randalls were seated at the breakfast table. John immediately stood and reached for Emma. "I'll hold her while you fix her bottle."

She didn't bother protesting. "Thank you."

"Lucy," Camille began, "I want you to know that we realize how disturbed your husband is, but we are not going to let him touch you."

Lucy felt her eyes fill with tears. "Camille, it's not something you should have to do."

"I know, dear, but we as a family feel it's our duty to protect you and Emma." She rose and went to the stove. "Now, let me fix you some breakfast. You can eat while John feeds Emma." John had already gotten the bottle.

"Camille, you don't need to fix me anything," Lucy said. "I can eat cereal."

"No, you need a good breakfast."

Griff smiled at Lucy. "Let her cook for you. That's her way. Besides, she's a really good cook."

"I know she is. I'm just not sure she should cook for me. I'm not sure why any of you are doing what you're doing for me."

"Well, we know," Camille said. "Because we care about you." Then she brought a plate full of eggs and bacon to Lucy. "Eat every bit of this. You need to build your strength."

"Thank you, Camille," Lucy whispered.

Camille leaned over and hugged Lucy. "Thank you for staying."

Lucy nodded, but didn't speak because tears were filling her eyes.

"Now, eat up," Camille said. "Look at Emma! She's certainly not hesitating to do that."

"I'm thinking this bottle may not be enough," John said as Emma finished the last of her milk. "How about another half bottle?"

"Do you think so?" Lucy asked, looking at Camille.

"I don't think it would hurt. I'll get it while you eat, Lucy."

Lucy didn't say anything. She ate her breakfast, a large meal by her standards. But she kept an eye on her daughter. Emma did eat a little more, then she fell asleep.

"I'll put her in bed," Lucy said, jumping up from her chair.

"Okay," John said. "But come back. I have a question to ask you."

Lucy took her child and carried her to bed. She didn't want to do as John had asked; it seemed risky to her. But she gave in to his request.

"She's sound asleep," she announced as she reached the kitchen.

"That's good," John said. "Say, have you ever been horseback riding?"

"Oh, no, John, not this soon after giving birth," Camille protested.

"I just thought since I had the day off, it would be a good time for you to try something fun and get out into the fresh air."

"I think it might be too soon, John, but thank you for thinking of me."

"I can take another day off later, when you're ready."

"I'm not—not used to horses. I might not ever need to learn to ride, anyway. I probably won't stay on a ranch. I'll move in with Melissa and Harry, or find my own place to live."

"Really?" John asked in surprise. "I think a ranch is a great place to live and raise kids."

"But that's because you grew up on a ranch. That wasn't how I was raised."

"That's true," Camille joined in. "But you may

decide it's nice, after you've been here awhile. Change takes time, John. You should know that."

"Yeah," John agreed, but the expression on his face didn't look happy. "How about I take the four-wheeler and you go with me?" he suddenly asked, surprising Lucy.

"A four-wheeler?"

"Yeah. I can show you some of the ranch without you having to ride a horse. Will you come with me?"

Lucy could feel herself weakening. After losing one last effort to resist, she finally consented. "But I can't leave Emma for too long."

"We'll just be out a couple of hours. Back in time for lunch. Mom can take care of Emma for that long."

"You know I'd love to take care of Emma, Lucy. And I'll have Griff to help me, won't I, dear?"

Griff nodded.

"Well, I—I suppose I can go," Lucy stammered, "but just for a couple of hours."

"Great. Put on some warm clothes and I'll go get the four-wheeler. I'll drive it up to the door so you can just wait here for me."

John grabbed his coat and hurried out the door.

Lucy went back to her room, pulling a sweater over her shoulders and hoping her jeans would be warm enough. Then she grabbed her coat.

"Lucy, do you have any long underwear?" Camille called.

"No. Do you think I need them on under my jeans?"

"It wouldn't hurt. Here's a pair of mine. I think they'll work for you. And I have some gloves, too."

"Thank you, Camille. I didn't realize the undertaking would be so involved."

"You'll get used to it."

When she was ready to go, she found John had come in to get a small Thermos of coffee and some cookies.

"So you get just as hungry riding a four-wheeler as you do a horse?"

He chuckled. "No, not really, but I thought you might get hungry."

She couldn't hold back a smile. When John was amused, the entire world shone for Lucy.

"Ready?"

"Yes, if you are."

He escorted her out to the four-wheeler. "Have you ever been on one of these?"

"No. Are there seat belts?"

"No, honey, no seat belts. You just need to hold on to me. I won't go that fast today."

"Do you do a lot of your work from one of these?" she asked as he started the motor and drove away from the house.

"Not really. We use it in the open pastures, but not all of our land is flat. Besides, you can't round up cows on a four-wheeler, and you certainly can't cut out a cow from a herd with this machine."

"Do you do all those things?"

"Yeah, some days. That's why I ride most days."

"I'd like Emma to learn to ride when she's older."

"Then you'll have to ride, too."

"I will?"

"Sure. She won't believe she can ride unless she sees you riding."

"But—"

"We'll get her a little pony, and a small horse for you to start off. You'll like it."

She forced herself to say, "If we're still here when she's old enough."

"I think you will be. Cecil can't terrorize you for long. Either he gives in, or he'll be destroyed. We don't live in a world where he can continue to threaten you."

"I hope that's true."

"It is." They rode in silence for a while, enjoying the scenery and the closeness. At the crest of the hill, John stopped and pointed at a picturesque lake. "In a couple months we'll be able to skate on that, then we can swim in it. Still, it can be pretty cold. It takes a brave person to get in the water. Do you think you'll be able to do that?"

"I don't know. I haven't been in a mountain lake."

"You'll like it. We can have a picnic on the banks of it."

"It's gorgeous. The kind of place you see in travel books."

"Yeah, except our lake is private. You and Emma are welcome anytime, Lucy. If you're not living on the ranch then."

"Thank you."

"Where did you grow up? Harry must've told me, but I've forgotten."

"I grew up in a small town in Colorado. But when Mom and Dad divorced, I went with her to Kansas City."

"Why did she go there?"

"She wanted to live in a big city, far away from Dad."

"Were you happy there?"

"I didn't ever find my comfort zone in Kansas City. Mom dated a lot, and I stayed home alone when she went out. I missed our small town, my friends. The girls at school were nice, but I didn't want to invite anyone over to my house. It was a rental and Mom didn't fix it up much. I was embarrassed."

"And Harry wasn't around?"

"No, he left for college and didn't come back to Mom's house. He worked through the summers and if he took any time off, he went to Dad's."

"Didn't he want to see you?"

"I was a shy twelve-year-old when he left home. Why would he want to see me?"

"It just seems a shame. I don't want to say anything bad about your mom, but she doesn't seem to have done a good job of raising you."

Lucy didn't like talking about her mother, nor thinking of her past. Her teenage years had been miserable, followed by several equally bad years at junior college. Then her mother had introduced her to Cecil. When she encouraged Lucy to marry him, Lucy had thought her mother should know about men. She hadn't thought about how her mother would save money if Lucy was married off.

That was a conversation Lucy had overheard on her wedding day.

From that time on, Lucy had never looked back. She threw herself into her life with Cecil—until he began to change. Shortly after their marriage, he stopped bothering with kindness or patience. And he started hitting her.

But she didn't want to think of her husband. She wasn't going back to him or their marriage.

"Lucy?"

She shook off her thoughts and looked at John. "Yes?"

"You seemed lost in thought."

"Just some unpleasant memories."

"I want you to see some of our cattle. The boys are moving a herd that you'll be able to see in just a minute when we top the next hill."

When they reached the top of the small hill, the acres of the ranch spread out before them. Lucy saw the herd of cattle John had talked about. "What are they called?"

"Those are Herefords."

"They're beautiful."

"In the spring, when they have their babies, you'd really like it. The baby calves are snow white on the head and deep red in their coats."

"I'd love to see them."

"You will, Lucy. But remember, they aren't pets. Don't get attached to any of them."

"Why?"

"Because some of them will be destined to become steaks. Understand?"

"Yes, I guess so."

"Want to go look at a herd of horses? You can fall in love with them. They'll be around and you can bond with your horse."

"All right."

"Hold on," he reminded her as he took off in another direction.

"Are you warm enough?"

"Yes." She might've given a nod to his mother if she was around. The long underwear under her jeans and the gloves made the cold bearable.

After they rode for about fifteen minutes, John slowed down and parked under a tree. He unscrewed the lid from the Thermos he'd brought and filled two paper cups for them.

"Do we get the cookies now, too?" she asked eagerly.

"Yeah, you get the cookies. I thought you might be feeling a little peckish about now. And you can look at the horses while you have a snack."

"Good. I hadn't noticed the horses until you said that. Do you think they'll come closer to us?"

"Yeah. They're social animals, if they're trained. And some of them will hope you'll share your cookies with them."

"I don't know about sharing the cookies," she said, thinking he was teasing her.

"We'll see," he said, smiling.

He was right. The horses soon surrounded their vehicle and John gave her some apples he'd brought to feed the horses.

"But what if they bite me?"

"They won't. Just hold the piece of apple flat in your hand. They'll pick it up."

She found he was right. Several of the horses came to her extended hand and nibbled the pieces of apple. She even was comfortable enough to pet them.

"Rub their noses. They're very soft."

"But won't they get upset?" she asked.

"Nope. They like it."

She again found that he was right.

Distracted by the animals, she scarcely noticed when she heard some music, until she realized it was John's cell phone. But she didn't pay it much attention.

John got off the phone and said, "I think we'd better go back. Cecil just phoned the sheriff's office asking for Harry."

"Where was he?"

"He said he was in Kansas City. The deputy told him Harry was out of town. Then he asked about you, but the deputy said he hadn't seen you."

Lucy drew a deep breath. "That was kind of him."

"Mike trains his guys pretty well. And he's taking your car from the mechanic's garage and putting it in his garage so it can't be seen around town."

"That's good," she said, ashamed that her voice was shaking.

"You're safe, Lucy. We're going to protect you."

"I—I know."

"Let's head back to the house. We've been gone long enough."

Lucy wasn't sure she'd be any safer in the house,

but she'd feel less vulnerable there. And she'd be with her baby. She wanted to make sure Cecil didn't get close to Emma.

When they reached the house, Griff told them Cecil hadn't been seen in Rawhide. Mike just wanted to let them know.

Lucy gave a shuddering sigh. "Emma?"

"She's not awake yet," Camille said.

"All right. I'll go check on her," Lucy said, excusing herself. Before she left the room, however, she remembered her manners. "I enjoyed our morning, John."

"Good. So did I."

GRIFF AND JOHN WENT to the barn after he and Lucy returned to the house. "Is she okay?" Griff asked.

John knew he meant Lucy. "I think so. She didn't say much but her voice was shaky."

"I see. There's something I've been meaning to tell you."

John looked at his father. "Yes?"

"Before we go back in, I feel like I need to mention something to you."

"What, Dad?"

"I got the impression Lucy was a little apprehensive of you this morning. Did you hug her or—or kiss her or something?"

John's cheeks flushed. "Yeah, I kissed her. She was worried about everything. I was just trying to calm her."

"Well, son, she's come from a marriage where her

husband hit her. She's going to be a little leery of getting close to anyone. Especially a man."

"But I'd never hit her, Dad!"

"Do you think her husband didn't promise to love and protect her when he married her?"

"Yeah, but—but she's so sweet and little."

"I know, but you're going to have to take it easy on her. She'll need time to adjust."

John knew his father was right. But he wondered how he'd last that long.

Chapter Eight

Four weeks later

Lucy rolled out of bed when her daughter woke her for her 4:00 a.m. feeding. It was nice, Lucy thought, to feel so good about life.

She'd been with the Randalls for over a month. Her health was really good now that she'd been eating a balanced diet, getting enough sleep and still managing to contribute to the household. It made her feel that she'd come a long way.

After fixing the bottle for Emma, Lucy settled down in the rocker in the den and fed her child. "Look at how much you've grown in a month, Emma. John can't really call you little Emma anymore, can he? I know he still does, but I'll have a talk with him, I promise. We don't want you to think that you're undersized."

Emma gurgled something that was masked by the nipple of her bottle. Not that they were words. Of course, she wasn't talking yet, but she did occasionally make noises that Lucy thought she could interpret.

"John's been very nice to me since I tried to run away. After that night, he hasn't gotten too close. That's good, isn't it, Emma? I mean, I didn't like being with your father, even though that's how I got you." Lucy stopped to think about that statement. "I think it's good that John's not interested…that he hasn't tried to kiss me again."

She'd thought about that kiss a lot. It hadn't been like Cecil's kisses, which hadn't come often. There was a sweetness to John's kiss that she hadn't experienced in quite a while. But she wasn't really interested in another relationship…was she?

She shook her head. "No, I wasn't shaking my head at you, sweetie. Wow, you finished your milk quickly, didn't you? Are you ready to go to sleep again? Then we'll get up at eight o'clock. All right, time for a burp."

She put Emma on her shoulder and gently patted her back. Emma responded as she had since her birth, with an enormous burp.

"Good girl, Emma. Mommy wants you to know you are absolutely perfect." Maybe her mother hadn't intended her to feel the weight of the world on her shoulders, but she had. Living here with the Randalls, Lucy had learned the power of believing in your goodness.

"I'm being a good mommy because that's what you deserve, Emma, my girl. I think that's important. Don't you?" She snuggled Emma to her and kissed her cheek. "Let's go back to sleep now, okay?"

She carried the baby back to her crib and tucked her in. Stepping back, she watched as Emma slowly drifted off. She loved watching her baby squirm and stir around for several minutes before she fell asleep.

With a sigh, Lucy headed to her bedroom. She loved waking up in the mornings in this room. It was a happy room and it helped her feel happy.

She got under the covers again and sighed as she put her head on her pillow.

JOHN ATE BREAKFAST with his men in the bunkhouse. He'd started doing that after his dad retired. There was no reason for his mother to get up just to fix his breakfast when the bunkhouse cook was already making a big meal for the cowboys.

And it made it possible for him to start his day without Lucy and Emma being a part of it, which helped him concentrate on the business at hand. Still, he'd found it difficult to keep his mind on the cows.

He always stopped by Emma's bed each morning at six to gently touch the baby. She was always sleeping soundly. He wanted to hold her, but he didn't wake her.

He'd paid attention to his father's warning about touching Lucy. He'd kept a friendly demeanor toward Lucy and given her some space. But he knew what he wanted. He wanted to hold her in his arms, to promise to protect her and Emma forever.

That would have to wait.

He'd just be her friend for now.

"I'D BETTER PUT IN some laundry, now that Emma's down," Lucy said.

She and Camille had just finished a cup of coffee on their afternoon break. The day had fulfilled its promise. Winter sunshine blazed through the window, and Caro had earlier pronounced Emma healthy and growing. The doctor visit had assured Lucy that she was doing her job.

"I swear, that child is getting bigger every day," Camille said, almost as if reading Lucy's mind.

"Caro says she's over ten pounds already." Lucy couldn't help but smile.

"When you went to Caro's, did you drive John's truck?"

Her smile faded. "Yes, he insisted. He doesn't want me to drive my car. He still thinks Cecil will be looking for me."

"It's possible, but I'd like to think he's moved on. I certainly hope so. I don't want him to have anything to do with you or Emma."

"Me, neither."

Lucy got the laundry started and then came to the kitchen to see if she could help with dinner. Under Camille's tutelage, she was learning how to cook. Now she could make a lot of Camille's recipes and John couldn't tell who prepared it.

It was getting close to John's arrival. Griff was working in his office. Lucy knew he would come to dinner when he heard John come in. She liked this time of the evening best, the coming together of all four of them to eat with one another and talk about their days.

When she got to the kitchen, she looked out the window to see John come out of the barn. "Oh, look, John's here early." The sight of him infused her with warmth. Tall and broad in his sheepskin jacket and cowboy hat, he was model handsome. She could still feel those arms as they'd held her.

She watched John walk toward the house, and her heart rate accelerated the closer he got. Suddenly he came to an abrupt halt.

Lucy followed John's gaze and almost passed out. There stood Cecil, with a gun pointed at John.

CECIL CALLED OUT in a loud voice. "Lucy? Where are you, Lucy? Come on out. I want to talk to you."

Lucy saw John turn to him, pretending confusion. "Who are you talking to?"

"I'm talking to my wife. I want to see her."

"She's not here, whoever she is. This is the Randall ranch."

Cecil looked angrier now. "I know that. But I found out you took in my wife. I want her back."

"You're mistaken."

"We'll find out. If she doesn't come out, I'll just shoot you."

Behind Lucy at the window Camille drew a deep breath. Then she turned to run to Griff's office.

Lucy heard Cecil cock his gun. She couldn't wait for Camille's return. She stepped out of the house.

"Here I am, Cecil," Lucy said.

Cecil swung around.

"I was right. There you are. Come on. I'm ready to go."

Lucy stood her ground. "I don't want to go with you, Cecil."

"You're my wife. You don't have a choice."

"Yes, I do."

She could see Cecil's face harden—a look she remembered all too well. "Okay, here's your choice. You come with me, or he dies." He pointed the gun at John.

"No! That's not fair. He's got nothing to do with this."

"Too bad. You've got until I count to three. One, two—"

"All right, I'm coming." She started toward him, willing to sacrifice herself for John. And for Emma. She'd never let him know the baby existed.

John's voice didn't stop her. "I don't think you should go with him."

"I'm not risking your life." Lucy hated Cecil, but this time she wasn't going to stay with him. One way or another, she would get away. Or die trying.

She only hoped John would protect Emma.

"Get in the car," Cecil said, keeping his gun on John.

After she got in, Cecil looked at her. "Maybe I should shoot him anyway. Why not?" He seemed to chuckle with evil glee.

"Because I'll kill you in return, Cecil."

His smug mirth died instantly. "What did you say?" Cecil asked, turning to look at her.

"I said if you take his life, your life will end shortly. I promise you that."

"Well, well, well. What happened to meek little Lucy? Did she go away?"

"Yes, she did." She raised her chin and looked at him defiantly. "Are you sure you want me back?"

"I'm sure. Okay, I won't shoot your friend." He opened the door on the driver's side and got in the car.

When he backed out of the long driveway, John came after him, but he didn't have a chance of catching them.

Lucy was only grateful that Cecil didn't hurt John.

She sat quietly beside Cecil as he started back toward Kansas City, a long drive back to hell.

Before they'd gone far, he asked, "What happened? Did you lose the baby?"

She went along with him. "Didn't you make sure of that?"

"I thought it was the best choice. Aren't you glad you don't have a crying kid around?"

"No, I'm not. I'll always hate you for what you did."

"And what about that cowboy?"

"What about him?"

"You like him?"

"More than I like you. But then that includes almost anyone I've ever met."

"You want me to pull over and give you a beating for your smart mouth?"

"I don't care, Cecil," she said, managing to control the shaking she'd shown in the past.

An hour down the road, Cecil stopped at a filling station to get gas. When he got out of the vehicle, Lucy opened her door and got out, too.

"What are you doing? Get back in the car!"

"No, I won't."

"Hell, yes, you will," Cecil said, raising his hand, as if she'd cower in fear.

But Lucy knew this was her opportunity. She stared at him and didn't even duck when his hand struck her across the face.

"Hey! You can't just hit her like that!" a man near them called out. "I'm calling the police." He pulled out a cell phone.

"She's my wife. I can hit her if I want."

"That's not true," a woman chimed in. "Go ahead and call the police. He can't get away with that!"

Cecil tried to grab Lucy and force her back into the car, but she fought him as hard as she could. She was stronger now than she used to be, she discovered. Or he was weaker.

When several men rushed toward them Cecil panicked and got in his car and drove away.

Lucy couldn't have been happier.

She didn't have any money to make a phone call. So she thanked the people who helped her and then started walking back toward Rawhide.

She didn't know how long it would take her to make up the hour's drive back to the Randall ranch. She just hoped Cecil didn't turn around and try to force her into his car. On alert she walked toward the ranch. Once she got there she would take Emma and disappear.

JOHN BARELY WAITED for Mike's pickup to stop before he jumped in the passenger seat and directed him down the road Cecil had taken. He'd wanted to chase the maniac himself but his father had made him wait for the sheriff, who was only minutes away.

"What happened?" Mike asked.

John told him of the events that had preceded his arrival.

"Sounds like a coward if there ever was one. Do you think he stuck to this road?"

"I think so. It's the most direct route to Kansas City. That's where he lives."

"Okay, we'll catch up with them soon."

Half an hour later, John yelled for Mike to stop.

Mike pulled off the road. "What is it?"

"It's Lucy! Back up!"

Mike did, almost hitting Lucy as she struggled alongside the road.

John swung his door open. "Lucy! What happened? Why are you out here walking?"

"I'm trying to get back to the ranch so I can take care of Emma."

"Why did you go with him in the first place?" John demanded, almost yelling.

"Because I couldn't protect Emma and allow him to shoot you. How terrible would I be to allow such a thing to happen?"

"He wasn't going to shoot me! He was threatening to do so, but he's too much of a coward to kill me."

"You don't know that! He cocked his gun. I couldn't stand there and take that chance. No! Never!"

Mike stepped between them. "Okay, you two. How about we get in the truck and head back to Rawhide. You can yell at each other once we get Lucy back home."

John escorted Lucy back to Mike's truck and held the door for her. Then he got in beside her, staring straight ahead.

"GRIFF, WHAT ARE WE going to do?" Camille asked her husband as she held Emma in her arms. "Will he hurt her?"

"He'll probably try. But Lucy is stronger now. I think she'll stand up to him."

"I hope so, but will she be able to get away? And where will she be? Will they catch them?"

"I don't know, sweetheart. We'll keep her in our prayers. And we'll take care of Emma. We know she loves Emma and will come back to her if she can."

"Yes, she loves Emma. And Emma loves her, right, Emma? Mommy will come back to you if she can. I promise."

"Will you be willing to let Emma go?"

"Go? Go where? Will Lucy have a safe place to take her?"

"I don't know. But will she want to stay here when Cecil knows where she can be found?"

"We can protect her, can't we?"

"We can try, but I don't know if we can do that without risking being hurt."

"When you went with your cousins into the mountains to find Jim and Patience and see if they needed your help, did you risk being hurt?"

"Yes, I did. And I'll risk myself again for Lucy and Emma. But will Lucy let us?"

"Is that her choice?"

"It is, but she put herself in harm's way to save John's life. I'm grateful to her for that sacrifice."

"Of course we are. But I want a happy ending for Lucy. She's such a good person. It seems to me that she's grown up a lot the past month."

"I think so, too. But I'm not sure about a happy ending—not as long as Cecil is alive."

"Someone just pulled into the drive," Camille said, jumping to her feet, Emma clutched in her arms.

"Stay here. I'll go see who it is." Griff hurried from the room.

It didn't take long for him to return. "It's John and Mike with Lucy!"

Camille met Lucy at the door and hugged her even as she handed over Emma. "She's fine, Lucy. I fed her."

"Thank you, Camille. I knew I could count on you and Griff keeping her safe."

"How did you get away from him? And where did you meet Mike and John?" Camille asked in a rush.

"I'll tell you later. Let me put Emma in bed first." Lucy took her baby and left the room.

"Well? Are you going to tell us, John? Where did you find her?"

"Walking down the road. She was planning to walk all the way back here."

"That poor dear. She must be starved to death! How about you, Mike?"

"I'm hungry, Camille, I can confess to that."

"I'll have dinner on the table in ten minutes." She rushed to the kitchen.

Griff looked at the two men. "How did she get away?"

Mike filled him in on the details as Lucy had explained.

"She's gotten tougher since she got here," Griff said with a grin. "I don't think she would've lasted so long if that had happened a month ago."

John silently agreed with his father. But a niggling fear lingered in his mind. Cecil knew where to find Lucy. And he doubted the maniac would stop till he had her.

Chapter Nine

Lucy gave thanks for her return to her baby. And the Randalls. She'd wondered if she'd seen the last of them when she'd had to leave with Cecil. He was a dangerous man. Also a stupid man, she'd finally realized.

Now she needed to make plans for the morning. She could allow herself one night here. Then she and Emma would disappear. She'd had five weeks in paradise. She mustn't be greedy.

After reaching out to pat her daughter's back, Lucy turned to leave the baby's room. She paused at the doorjamb to look back. It was such a pretty room. Too bad Emma wouldn't remember her first surroundings when she was older.

When Lucy got to the den, only the men were there.

"Where's Camille?" she asked.

"She's putting dinner on the table. I'm sure you're hungry, Lucy. You've had a hard day."

"Thank you, but I'll go help—"

"Dinner's ready," Camille announced. "Come on in and sit down."

Lucy hugged Camille before she went to sit down. "You put in a lot of extra work, Camille."

"Well deserved, Lucy. I knew you'd need a good meal."

After several minutes, Camille said, "What are we going to do? Do you think he'll come back?"

Mike put down his fork. "Yeah, Camille, I think he'll come back. Men who find a woman they can beat on don't easily give up on their victim."

"I'm not a victim anymore," Lucy said.

"He doesn't know that yet, Lucy," John said roughly. "You'll need to beat him at his own game to convince him of that."

"I'll take Emma and disappear," Lucy said, keeping her voice firm.

John put down his fork. "You promised you wouldn't run away."

"I promised I wouldn't sneak away in the middle of the night. I can tell you all goodbye and not be sneaking away."

"I don't think that's our best option," Mike said, interrupting John's angry response.

"What do you think is the best option?" Camille asked.

"To station deputies on the road into Rawhide from either direction. They'll give us enough time to set up outside. I'd like John to be one of my deputies. He's the best sharpshooter in the group."

"Sure, Mike, I'll help out."

"Why would you need a sharpshooter?" Lucy asked.

"If Cecil uses a gun again and gets control of you,

shooting him may be the only way to save you," Mike said solemnly. "You do realize that, don't you?"

"Surely if you pointed a gun at him, he'd surrender."

"Not necessarily," Mike said. "He might refuse to give up. I need someone to line up the shot, to make sure that you don't get hit."

"I don't think this will work, Mike." Lucy looked at the three Randalls, along with Mike. "I don't want any of you to get hurt. I don't think I could live with that happening."

"We're not going to get hurt, Lucy," Mike promised.

"Wouldn't it be better for me to find somewhere else to live?"

"You know Harry won't like that solution," John said.

"No, I don't know that. I haven't seen my brother since he came to Rawhide. We're not close. I came here because I needed some support, but he's not here. You've taken his place. You're the ones I have to worry about."

"I told you I was representing Harry," John said. "He's not only my brother-in-law. He's also my best friend."

"I don't want any of you hurt," Lucy protested again.

"Don't worry," Mike replied. "We'll make careful plans. You'll be fine and so will we. I promise."

She nodded. "Just keep that promise."

THE FIRST THING MIKE DID was make some calls to get deputies on the roads that led into Rawhide. While he suspected Cecil might come in from the south, the road that led to Kansas City, he wasn't taking any chances.

His next call was to his wife, Caroline, to let her know he wouldn't be home the rest of the night, or most of the next day, either.

Then he looked at John. "Are you sure you want to be the sharpshooter here? It might upset Lucy if you have to kill Cecil."

"I wouldn't want anyone else to be the sharp-shooter. I need to do that job."

Just then, Griff and Camille came into the living room.

"Have you got things set up?" Camille asked.

"Yes, we do. John and I are going to sleep here, so we'll be ready if my cell phone rings."

"You think he'll be back this soon?" Griff asked.

"I would, if I was him," Mike said simply.

"What can I do?" Griff said.

"Stay inside with Camille and Lucy. Keep them safe."

"Okay, I will, but you two be careful."

"Hey, we've already promised both ladies. We will."

"Okay, good night," Griff said as he and Camille left to go to bed.

THE CELL PHONE RINGING awakened Mike. He sat up, shaking his head, reaching for John's shoulder as he answered the phone.

"Yeah? Okay, thanks."

John stared at his companion in the shadowy room. "It's him?"

"Yeah. They just saw him drive by. He should be here in about fifteen minutes."

"Okay." John stood up.

"Be sure to get your coat, John. It's cold out there

in the early morning. The sun won't be up for at least another half hour."

"I didn't figure Cecil for an early riser," John said, yawning.

"Me, neither, but we want to be prepared."

The two men put on their coats and got their weapons. Then they slipped outside and took their positions.

John's finger was steady on the trigger.

The best shot, he knew, was a head shot. And if it came to that, he didn't plan to miss.

CECIL HATED being up so early. But he wasn't going to let Lucy go that easily. He had a job to do. After a few hours' sleep at the first motel he'd come to, he went to a store to buy chloroform, then gathered some cloths to put it in. Now he was prepared. He was going to sneak in that house before anyone else was up and drag Lucy out.

She wasn't getting away again.

That cowboy who thought he was so tough would be asleep the whole time. Cecil chuckled. He wouldn't even be awake to rescue her.

Not much amused Cecil, but that thought did. When the cowboy woke up, Lucy would be gone. He could imagine her pitiful cries because she knew he would make her pay for running away.

He believed in making her pay. That's why he'd hit her the second time. She'd gotten pregnant. He didn't want to be pestered by any children. And he didn't want his wife occupied by a child. He wanted her attention on him.

"Oh, yeah," he said aloud.

He didn't pull into the drive of the Randall ranch. Instead he sat there, on a darkened road, biding his time till the moment was right.

LUCY WAS DEEP IN SLEEP when something woke her. She could just see the hint of light through the window. Was that what had awakened her? She looked around her bedroom.

She had just decided everything was fine, when she noticed a shadow in her room. In her sleep-dazed mind, she couldn't quite imagine what it was. Then it dawned on her. Cecil was in her bedroom. Before she could scream for help, he placed a cloth over her nose.

Her last thought was that she was glad she'd closed Emma's door.

THE CHLOROFORM knocked her out, just as he'd planned.

Cecil slung Lucy over his shoulder. Then he stumbled. She'd put on weight, he thought. He struggled through the house to the back door where he'd broken in just before sunrise.

His plan was great, except getting Lucy back to the car. Now he wished he hadn't left his car out on the road. And because he'd thrown her on his shoulder, he couldn't keep the cloth over her nostrils. As he got to the back door, she began fighting him, in a sluggish manner.

Pulling out a gun, he placed it to her head. "I'll shoot you if you don't stop. I've got a gun pointed at your head."

She slumped, showing she understood, but she

became a dead weight, dragging him down. Cecil grabbed her arms and tried to sling her over his shoulder again.

Her head hit the edge of the door as he got her outside the house. He was breathing heavily, but maybe she'd stay knocked out. He didn't have far to go.

"Halt, Cecil!"

He came to a stop and peered through the slowly brightening air. The sheriff stood twenty yards away.

"Put her down."

"I've got a gun, and I'll shoot her before you can get over here, so just keep your distance." Cecil slung Lucy around in front of him and pressed his gun to her head again.

"Cecil, you're breaking the law. You need to drop the gun and put Lucy down on the ground."

Instead, Cecil started toward the driveway.

"Cecil, I'm warning you. You need to stop."

Cecil just walked faster, going backward and dragging Lucy.

"John." Mike's voice was almost hushed, but Cecil heard it. Just before the rifle shot.

LUCY CAME AWAKE with a sudden jolt of her body hitting the ground as Cecil fell.

She sat up, rubbing her head. Mike was there before she had a chance to realize what had happened. "Come on, Lucy, let's get you back where it's warm."

She stared up at him, confusion reigning on her face. Then she realized she was only wearing her nightgown. "Where are my clothes? What am I doing out here?"

"Cecil came to get you. He thought he'd outsmarted us by sneaking in just before dawn. He didn't drive down the driveway like we thought he would."

"Where is he?" she asked. Then she saw his legs underneath her and automatically tried to turn to look at him, but Mike held her head to keep her from looking. "Come on, Lucy. We've got to get you in the house."

He scooped her up and handed her to John. "Take her inside."

Lucy tried to squirm around in a position to see Cecil, but John shielded her from seeing the man until he stopped to open the back door. Then Lucy got a clear view of the mass in the driveway that had once been Cecil.

A small moan slipped through her lips.

John didn't stop. Once he got her through the door, he continued on into the kitchen. He set her down at the breakfast table. "I'll go get your robe."

She sat there with her eyes closed, seeing again that view of Cecil, her stomach roiling. Just as John got back to her, she rushed to the sink and lost what was in her stomach.

John helped her into her robe and led her back to the table. "Sit down, Lucy. I'll get you some water."

As he moved, his father came running into the room. "Lucy, are you all right?"

"She's fine, Dad," John answered.

"Did Cecil come? What happened to your plan?"

"He didn't pull in the driveway. He slipped into the house and used chloroform to knock Lucy out. Then he tried to drag her out of the house. She started coming to, so he pulled a gun and held it to her head."

"So you—" Griff stopped himself in time, but he looked at John.

John nodded his head and tried to get Lucy to drink some water. "I'm sure it's the gas he used that made you sick," he told her.

"No. No, I saw him," she muttered.

Then, like an approaching rainstorm rolling in, Lucy's composure shattered. She began sobbing.

"Should I wake up Camille?"

"No, Dad, I'll take care of her."

John took her on his lap and put her head on his shoulder and let her cry. He held her tightly, soothing her as she cried. When the tears lessened, he said, "You're safe, Lucy. Cecil can never hurt you again. We gave him several chances, but he was so arrogant he thought he could get away with it. He didn't believe Mike's warning."

"B-but wasn't there any other way?"

"Yes. He could've given up. But he wouldn't do that…"

"Thank you for saving me."

"I told you I'd keep you safe. You mean too much to me."

She sat there on his lap, unaware of anything else for several minutes.

Griff heard a vehicle in the driveway and went to the back window. "It's one of Mike's deputies. Oh, there are two of them. They brought out— Never mind. They're cleaning things up."

John stood. "I'll go out and talk to Mike."

"JOHN SHOT HIM IN THE HEAD?" one of the deputies said as he stared at the body on the driveway.

"He didn't have a lot of choice. The man was holding Lucy in front of him with a gun to her head, dragging her backward down the driveway."

"That took a lot of nerve," the other deputy said.

"Yeah, it did," John agreed.

"That's why you're the best shot I know, John," Mike said. "Did you get Lucy inside okay?"

"She caught a glimpse of the body as we went in. She threw up, but I didn't know if it was from seeing what was left of him, or the chloroform."

"I'm sure she'll recover when she has time to think about what happened. She wouldn't have come back alive if he'd gotten her this time."

"Yeah, I know."

"You remember that I warned him. He didn't think I meant it. He thought he had the power because he had a gun. He's the one who forced the issue."

"I know."

"I'll make sure Lucy knows, too."

"You ought to give her a little nap first. She doesn't get up this early. She feeds Emma at four and then sleeps until her next feeding at eight."

"Ah, I didn't realize she didn't usually get up early."

"No, she's not an early person right now."

"She sure is a lot prettier than when she first came to town," one of the deputies said with a grin.

John turned to glare at the man.

He shrugged. "I didn't mean anything by that. I just thought— Never mind."

"She's a new mother. And now a widow, thanks to me. You need to keep those things in mind."

"Yeah, especially the widow part," the other deputy said, snickering.

"I'm going to knock your head off if you keep making stupid remarks like that," John growled.

"And if you need any references, ask the mess you're scraping off the driveway," Mike drawled.

The two deputies ducked their heads and got on with what they were there for. It wasn't long before they loaded the body bag into the SUV and headed back to town.

"Okay, let's go see if Lucy is still up," Mike suggested.

When they got to the kitchen, they found Griff there with his hands wrapped around a steaming mug. He got up and poured them coffee as soon as he saw them coming in the door.

"Drink your coffee," he told them. "I'll cook breakfast for you."

"Did Mom take Lucy back to her bedroom?" John asked.

"Yeah. She thought she'd feel better if she got a little more sleep."

In a couple of minutes, all three were eating Griff's bacon and eggs.

"Don't tell Camille, but you cook almost as good as her," Mike said as he ate his last bite.

"I heard that," Camille said as she joined them.

"You didn't go back to bed?" Griff asked.

"I couldn't sleep."

"How is Lucy?" John asked.

"Resting. Hopefully, when she gets up later, all the chloroform will be out of her system."

"We hope so, Camille," Mike said. "He fooled us, sneaking in without driving his vehicle up the driveway. We were quite surprised when he came out of the house with Lucy in his arms."

"You knew she hadn't gone willingly. He held that rag over her nose until she passed out. He left the rag in her bed."

"Did you get it out of there?" John asked.

"Yes, of course. I didn't want it around Lucy when she woke up."

"Or Emma, either," Griff mentioned. "Luckily, Cecil never knew he had a baby. He might've killed Emma while he stole Lucy away."

"I know it's not nice to say, but I'm glad he's dead," Camille said. "Anyone who would try to hurt Lucy and her baby doesn't deserve to live."

All three men agreed.

"Will Lucy think that way, though?" John asked.

"Yeah, she will." Mike stood up. "I'm going to go home now, but I'll be back out about nine o'clock and talk to her. It will be all right, John."

John was grateful for his friend's reassurance, though he wasn't sure he fully agreed.

He and Griff stood to shake his hand.

"We can't thank you enough, Mike," Griff said.

"I think John had as much to do with it as me. I'll see you around nine."

"Thanks, Mike," John added as he walked to the door.

Once the man had left, the three Randalls sat down around the kitchen table.

"Do you think Lucy will be okay?" Camille asked, looking for more assurance.

Griff reached over and patted his wife's hand. "She'll be fine. Lucy is no dummy. I suspect she'll realize John saved her life."

"Maybe," John muttered. "I should probably go saddle up."

"I think you can afford to skip today, son," Griff said. "Maybe stay here and feed Emma a bottle."

"I could give her her eight o'clock and let Lucy sleep a little longer," John suggested, his voice perking up.

"That's a good idea, John," Camille said. "But you'll need to get her before she stirs, or she'll wake up Lucy."

"Yeah. I'll go in and get her up a few minutes before eight. I'll change her diaper and bring her in here before she can cry for her mama."

"She doesn't much cry for anyone when you have her, son," Griff reminded him. "It's like she knows who you are."

"I think she just likes the sound of my voice."

Camille stood up. "I think I'll fix me some breakfast. Would either of you like anything else?"

"You going to make pancakes?" Griff asked.

"I suppose I could. It wouldn't take long to mix up some batter."

"I'd like some, too," John said.

"You two are bottomless pits," Camille said with a smile.

LUCY STRETCHED, wondering why Emma hadn't woken her up. She checked her watch and discovered it was eight-thirty.

With a frown, she sat up. And then she remembered.

Cecil had come to get her. He'd knocked her out and dragged her out of the house. And then a bullet had pierced his head.

She closed her eyes, reliving that moment. She hadn't realized what had happened until she got a look at Cecil's body in the driveway.

He was definitely dead.

But what had happened to Emma? Lucy slipped out of her bed and wrapped her robe around her to hurry next door to Emma's room.

No Emma.

Then she heard voices in the den. She hurried there to discover her baby in John's arms, cooing to him as he talked to her.

The tender sight was enough to make her feel dizzy. She turned around and returned to bed.

Chapter Ten

She was a widow.

The fact hit Lucy as she put Emma to bed later that morning.

Cecil was dead—and she was free. Free to live her life without fear. Free to raise Emma without worry that someday the maniac would return.

But did Cecil have to die to accomplish that? Seeing his lifeless body had affected her more than she'd thought. There was a pain in the pit of her stomach that she doubted would go away anytime soon.

Assured that Emma was asleep, she went to the den where she heard Camille talking to Mike Davis.

"How are you, Lucy?" Mike asked after greeting her.

"I'm fine," she lied. "I don't think there's any chloroform left in me." That at least was true.

"Have you eaten?"

"No, I—"

"Let me fix you some pancakes," Camille protested, getting up to go to the kitchen.

"No, Camille, I'm not sure I can eat anything."

Camille ignored her protest. "It'll just take a minute. I'll fix you some, too, Mike."

"Thanks, but I'll just take a cup of coffee."

After he watched Camille leave, Mike turned back to Lucy. "You realize you weren't going to make it back alive if we hadn't saved you, don't you?"

"Yes, I realize that."

"So you know John saved your life?"

"Yes."

"So you're all right with what happened?"

Lucy looked down at her hands, clenched in her lap. "Yes. There should've been a better way, but—"

"But Cecil didn't give us a choice."

"You tried to get him to let me go?"

"Three times I told him he was breaking the law and he needed to let you go. He ignored me and tried to drag you after him, using your body as a shield."

"That's why John shot him in the head?"

"He didn't have a choice. He wasn't going to take a chance of hurting you."

Lucy kept her gaze on her hands. "I know."

"Breakfast is ready, Lucy," Camille announced. "And your coffee is hot, too, Mike."

"Okay. Where are Griff and John?"

"They went to the barn to check on a calf there." Camille put Mike's coffee in front of him.

Lucy sat down at the table, unsure if she would be able to eat. Her stomach still wasn't settled.

"Just try, Lucy," Camille whispered as she put the plate of pancakes in front of her.

Slowly, Lucy picked up her fork and cut into the

pancakes, after she'd added a little syrup. Managing to swallow the first bite, she was surprised when hunger attacked her. She reached for a second bite, loving the way it filled the hollow in her stomach.

"Good job, Lucy," Mike said softly, giving her a smile. "You need to eat so you can be strong for Emma."

Just then they heard the two men come in the back door. When they got to the kitchen, they both smiled at Lucy, who was swallowing the last bite of breakfast.

"Good job, Lucy," Griff said. "We were worried about you getting some food down you."

"These pancakes awakened my hunger," Lucy assured him. She noticed John look at Mike, a question in his gaze.

Mike nodded, to let John know everything was all right.

"Well, now that I've finished my coffee, I guess I'd better get back to town."

Both Randall men shook his hand again, offering their thanks. Lucy swallowed a bite of pancakes and stood, also, extending her hand. "Thank you, Mike, for finding a way out for me. I appreciate it."

"I hope you've thanked John. He's the only man here who could've made that shot."

She turned to John and swallowed the lump in her throat. "Yes, thank you, John. I know—it was a difficult thing to do. But I'm grateful you saved me."

She hadn't loved Cecil much when she'd married him, and she had hated him by the time she'd left him. Still, she would've preferred a way out without killing him.

But it had come down to him or her, and she was glad she was the winner.

THAT AFTERNOON, when the phone rang, Camille answered it.

"Wonderful. Tomorrow at twelve-forty? Probably Griff will come. I don't know about anyone else. But you can come here for supper. We'll want to hear all about your trip and you'll need to meet Lucy and Emma."

After a moment, she said goodbye.

"Lucy, that was Melissa. She and Harry are coming in tomorrow afternoon. Isn't that great?"

"Yes, of course. I'd better pack our things."

"What? Why would you do that?"

"Aren't you sending me home with them?"

"No, Lucy. I think you should stay here with us. Melissa and Harry are a great couple, but they don't notice anyone else. I think you'll be better off here with us."

"I don't want to add to your burdens, Camille."

"You're not a burden, and Emma is a continual delight. I swear, I've gotten younger just holding her!"

"Oh, Camille, you are so kind. But I'm not sure—"

"At least wait until we talk to Melissa and Harry."

"Okay, I'll wait. But I'm not sure—"

"I am. Isn't it almost time for Emma's bottle again? I'll be glad to feed her if you have something else to do."

"I do need to fold clothes," Lucy said, knowing that was what Camille wanted to hear. But in her head, Lucy was trying to think what she should do. She could understand why Harry and Melissa might not want her in their house. But she wasn't sure where she could go. She'd have to have a babysitter taking care of her baby while she held down a job.

She didn't look forward to leaving her child.

Could she trust someone to take care of Emma? Could she find a job in Rawhide or go back to Kansas City? With Cecil's death, she could do that. Suddenly her life was in a tailspin. She felt as if she'd lost her sense of direction.

She wasn't sure Harry's arrival would make a difference in her life. She wanted to get to know her brother again. But if he wasn't interested, she could go away. Make her own life, for her and Emma.

Except that she didn't have much money. Just the seven hundred dollars she'd had with her when she got to town. And she hadn't paid any bills…because none had been presented. What could she do about that? Did she go to the hospital and ask for a bill that she knew she couldn't pay?

Confusion reigned. That night, Lucy didn't sleep well. Even as she fed Emma, she couldn't sleep afterward. She'd finally dozed after an hour or so, only to wake up two hours later. By the time Emma woke her for her eight o'clock bottle the next morning, Lucy was exhausted.

When she reached Emma's bed, she found John changing Emma's diaper.

"What are you doing?"

John didn't turn around. "What does it look like?"

"Why aren't you riding out today?"

"I'm going with Dad to meet Melissa and Harry's plane."

"Oh. I didn't know."

He picked up Emma and turned to face her. "What's wrong with you?" he asked, staring at her.

"I didn't sleep very well."

"Go back to bed. I'll take care of Emma."

"Are you sure?"

"Emma and I are pals. Of course I'm sure."

"All right." She leaned toward John and kissed her baby before she went back to her bedroom, to crawl into bed and close her eyes.

"DAD! JOHN! THANK YOU for coming to get us!" Melissa exclaimed, offering them both hugs.

Harry hugged them both, too. He loaded their luggage in the back of the SUV before getting in.

Griff drove out of the Casper airport and headed for Rawhide.

"So how's Lucy and the baby?" Harry asked.

"She's fine," John said. "And Emma is a darling."

"She's healthy?"

"Yeah, Harry, she's great."

"Has her ex-husband been heard from?" Melissa asked.

There was a silence for several minutes. Then John told them about the recent event.

"I owe you, John, for saving Lucy."

"I did it for Lucy, Harry. She deserves to live without that man threatening both her and Emma. He died not even knowing about Emma. Lucy didn't want him to know."

"Good. Is she traumatized by what has happened?"

"I'm not sure. She didn't sleep well last night. When she got up this morning she didn't look good."

"She doesn't blame you, does she?" Melissa asked.

"She says not."

"Dad? What do you think?"

"I think Lucy could use a little time to realize what has happened."

"But she can't blame John!" Melissa protested.

"Sis, she's suffered a lot in the past month or two. She's not blaming me. She just has to find her own way through all of this."

"Well, we won't stand for her blaming you!"

"Missy, we have to be fair to Lucy, as well as John," Harry said, using his wife's pet name. "You have to remember the man beat her in her eighth month of pregnancy."

"I know. That's why she should be glad that he's dead!"

John looked over his shoulder at his sister. "Melissa, you need to be gentle with Lucy. She hasn't done anything wrong."

"We'll see," she said, determined to support John.

Griff cleared his throat. "Your mom wants Lucy to stay with us, even though you're back home."

"Why?" Harry wanted to know.

"She says you two aren't even aware of anyone else. That Lucy would be really lost if she lived with the two of you." Griff added, "I think she may be right."

"Daddy!" Melissa protested.

"Well, you don't seem to notice anyone else when the two of you are together."

"I can't leave my sister at your place, Griff," Harry said. "That wouldn't be fair."

"Have you thought about taking the baby away from Camille? She's enjoying herself taking care of Emma."

"She's not her grandbaby," Melissa said.

"You tell her that and you'll discover a mama bear protecting her young," Griff warned. "She may not be, but we like to think of her as our grandchild. She doesn't seem to have any other grandparents."

"But what if we have a child?" Melissa asked.

"You got news for us, little girl? We can have more than one grandchild."

"I— We'll wait until we come for dinner and talk then." Melissa lay her head on her husband's shoulder.

They all rode in silence for about fifteen minutes. Then Harry asked about the sheriff's office business for the past six weeks.

John filled him in with what he knew. When he looked back to Harry, he realized his sister was asleep. "Is she okay?" he asked softly.

"Yeah. She's just a little tired. Traveling can do that. She hasn't been sleeping well."

"Mom hired some cleaning ladies to work on your house. It should be in good shape when you get there."

"Great. Be sure to thank her for us."

"Yeah, we will," Griff assured his son-in-law.

Melissa didn't stir as they pulled up at the house on

the back street of Rawhide that her father had bought from Caro and Mike.

Harry shook her awake. "Honey, wake up. We're home."

She groaned and fluttered her eyes.

He kissed her. "Wake up, Melissa. We're home again, finally."

JOHN AND GRIFF DECIDED not to say anything in front of Lucy.

"Hi, honey, we're home," Griff called as he entered the house. When he got to the kitchen, he discovered Lucy there helping Camille prepare Melissa and Harry's homecoming dinner.

"You met them?" Camille asked, obviously anxious.

"Sure we did. They were doing fine. Except they were both pretty tired. Melissa fell asleep on the way home. Harry was pouring her a glass of milk as we left their house."

Camille jerked her head up. "Milk? Melissa was drinking milk?"

"That's right, honey. That's what she asked for."

"Is she pregnant?" Camille asked at once.

"She said she and Harry would talk to you when they got here tonight," Griff said.

"And you didn't think that meant something?"

"Mom, you can't assume—" John began.

"Yes, I can. I think she's pregnant!"

"You'll have to wait until this evening, sweetheart."

"What brought up the subject?" Camille demanded.

Griff and John looked at each other and then looked away.

"Griff?" Camille prodded.

"Uh, Lucy, could you excuse us for a minute?"

Lucy stared at Griff. Then she nodded and walked out of the kitchen.

Griff nodded at John. He followed Lucy out of the kitchen. "Are you going to check on Emma?" John asked Lucy as she walked through the den.

"I thought I would. It's almost four o'clock."

"Mind if I go with you? I haven't seen her in three or four hours."

"You spend more time than that in the saddle every day."

"Yeah, but I always miss Emma. And you."

"Me? What are you talking about?"

"Nothing. I just miss talking to you and Emma. That's all."

"You know I can't stay here, don't you?"

"No, I don't know that."

"Look, John, I can't live off your parents now that Harry and Melissa are back. I've got to go someplace. I don't know where, but I can't let your parents support me."

"Honey, don't you realize money isn't a problem for my parents?"

"That doesn't matter. I need to pay my own way. I'm going to get a job."

"But who will take care of Emma?"

Lucy looked away. "I don't know. I'll have to find someone who can take care of her while I work."

"Mom could do that."

"What?"

"I said Mom could take care of her."

"But she wouldn't let me pay her."

"So? That's no reason to leave Emma with strangers."

"I need to be independent," Lucy said as she entered Emma's nursery.

"I think you'll hurt Mom's feelings with that argument. Is that what you want to do?"

"Of course not! I owe Camille so much. There's no way I could repay her."

"You know how much she loves Emma. Letting her take care of your baby would be a gift."

"John, I can't make a decision about that when I don't even know what I will be doing or where I'll be living."

"You think you're moving away? Why?"

"I don't know!" Lucy exclaimed, tears in her eyes. "I don't know anything. But I'm guessing that's why your dad wanted to talk to Camille without me there. And why you came after me to make sure I couldn't hear anything they said."

John couldn't argue with her. "Okay, let's wait until after tonight. But remember, you won't leave without saying goodbye."

"I'll remember."

Emma stirred, as if their fierce whispering had disturbed her. She tried to lift her head.

"Sorry for waking you up, Emma," Lucy cooed. "How are you? Are you ready for a new bottle?" Lucy asked.

"Hey, Emma. It's good to see you waking up," John added. He reached out to touch her cheek. She turned her head, moving her mouth toward his finger.

"Don't bite me, Emma!" John teased.

Lucy changed Emma's diaper. Then lifted Emma against her shoulder.

"May I go to the kitchen to fix her bottle, or should I wait?"

"I think you can go back. I'll go with you. I can make her bottle while you sit at the table and wait."

"All right."

They walked quietly until they could hear his parents still talking about something.

"We're coming to fix Emma's bottle," John called out.

Lucy said nothing.

When they reached the kitchen, Camille wore a welcoming smile. Griff smiled at them, too.

"Thanks for the advance warning," Camille said. "But it wasn't necessary."

"Mom, she already guessed you needed to talk without her hearing. I figured there was no need to take chances."

"Melissa was out of humor. That's what Griff wanted to tell me. I don't know what's wrong with her, but we'll find out tonight. I'm anxious for you to meet her."

"Yes, I'm anxious to meet her and to see Harry again."

"And this little girl is anxious to eat," John said as he came to the table with a bottle.

"Here you go, Lucy. It's all ready."

"Thank you, John. I'll go in the den and—"

"No, sit here with us. I'll fix you a glass of iced tea," John said, interrupting her. "Why not visit for a while?"

"I don't want to be in the way," Lucy said, trying to sound nonchalant, though she felt anything but.

Camille looked at her. "You could never be in the way, Lucy."

Somehow Lucy doubted that.

Chapter Eleven

John hoped his sister wasn't difficult tonight. He was afraid she was pregnant and wanted to replace Emma in his parents' hearts. He didn't want that to happen. They had room for more than one baby. But he feared Lucy would be hurt if that happened.

When six-thirty arrived, he heard his sister and brother-in-law at the back door. They came in before he could get to the door. He greeted them both and led the way into the breakfast area.

Lucy had been in the kitchen, but she wasn't now. He wondered where she'd gone. "Where's Lucy?" he asked his dad quietly as Camille was greeting her daughter and Harry.

"She went to comb her hair," Griff said. "I think it was an excuse to let Camille greet her daughter alone."

"I'll go—"

"No. She'll be back in a minute."

So John stood there waiting for Lucy's reappearance. As his father had said, Lucy slipped into the room without much notice. She immediately started putting dishes on the table.

When Camille noticed Lucy's activity, she called on her to meet her daughter.

"I'm pleased to meet you, Melissa. Hello, Harry."

Harry came around the table and hugged Lucy. "I'm sorry I wasn't here when you arrived. But I'm sure Camille and Griff did all that was necessary."

"Yes, they've been wonderful."

"I had no idea you were so pretty," Melissa said.

"Nothing to compare to you, Melissa. I can see how you drew Harry's attention at once."

"Why, thank you, Lucy. Where is your baby?"

"She's sleeping right now, but she'll be up around eight o'clock for a bottle if you don't mind waiting until then."

"Oh, no, not at all. I wouldn't want to disrupt her schedule."

"I think dinner is ready, everyone," Camille called, herding her family to the table. "What a nice table we have with Melissa and Harry back."

"Thanks for getting our place all cleaned and ready. And for the groceries, too. It was nice to have things there," Melissa said.

"Oh, I just made a phone call, dear."

"I'm going to hire Macey to clean for me full-time," Melissa said. "I think I'll be more productive working on my jewelry."

Lucy smiled at her sister-in-law. "Oh, I'd forgotten you make jewelry. Did you make what you're wearing? It's beautiful."

"Thank you. Yes, I made these." She touched her earrings.

John smiled. He hadn't realized how good Lucy would be, complimentary, relaxed, cordial, as the newlyweds entertained with stories about their European trip. Finally, over dessert, Harry turned the conversation to Lucy.

"So what do you plan on doing now, Lucy?"

Before Lucy could answer, Camille said, "I want her to stay here with us."

"Oh, Mom, we have news for you," Melissa said, beaming at her mother.

"What would that be, Melissa?"

"We're pregnant!"

"That's wonderful, dear, but that would make it all the more important that Lucy and Emma stay here."

Melissa stared at her mother. "I'm sure we could make room for them."

"I'll be excited to have *another* grandbaby, dear," Camille pointed out. "But Lucy is like my daughter, and Emma is the dearest thing. You'll love her."

"Of course," Melissa said.

"I was with Lucy when she gave birth to Emma. We count both of them as part of our family," John said.

"What do you mean, you were with her?" Harry asked.

"Well, Lucy didn't know anyone but me and she asked me to stay by her side," John explained.

"Why?" Harry seemed determined to get all the details.

"Because she was scared. I held her hand during the delivery. And I gave Emma her first bottle."

"You're not breast-feeding?" Melissa interjected. "I heard it's best for the baby."

Lucy didn't say anything.

Harry looked at his sister. "Melissa didn't mean to criticize you, Lucy."

"It's all right. I made my choice because I wasn't sure I would survive to feed her. It seemed more important to make sure someone could take care of her without me being there."

Melissa stared at Lucy. "You—you thought your husband would kill you?"

"Yes."

"And he tried," John pointed out. "Mike said if he got her away a second time, she wouldn't survive."

"I didn't realize—" Melissa began.

"It's all right, Melissa," Griff said. "We don't want to talk about those things. But Emma is a happy baby."

"But you haven't said what you want to do," Harry said. "Do you want to stay here with Camille and Griff?"

"I would never want them to feel unappreciated. They've been wonderful to me. But I think I need to stand on my own for my own growth. I married Cecil after only two years of college. I've never held down a real job. But I may need a little financial help in the beginning. I can pay back a loan as soon as possible."

"Lucy, money isn't a problem," Harry assured her. "But it won't be easy. Do you want to stay here in Rawhide?"

"I'd like to, if—if my being here won't cause problems."

John almost laughed out loud as everyone's gaze, except Lucy's, went to Melissa.

Fortunately, Melissa realized she was the only one who would keep Lucy from staying in Rawhide. "Oh, no, Lucy, I wouldn't want you to leave. I hope we can get to know each other."

"I can find another small town and—"

"No, of course not. Why not have more family in Rawhide?" Melissa grinned. "Just don't be surprised at having so much family."

"I don't think I can claim the Randalls, though they are very impressive, but I would like the chance to get to know Harry again, and you, my only sister-in-law."

"We'd love that, too. And you can help me get through my pregnancy and show me how to care for my baby."

"Thank you, Melissa. That's very generous of you," Lucy said, quietly wiping away the tears that flooded her eyes.

John wanted to wrap his arms around Lucy. But he feared she'd reject him if he tried. But he was so proud of her.

"I think you should stay here, Lucy," Camille said, "at least for a little while. Emma is only six weeks old."

"I know, but a lot of women go back to work even earlier," Lucy said.

"Give us at least two more weeks," Griff suggested. "That will give us all a little time to adjust to your departure."

"Of course, Griff. That's very generous of you and

I appreciate it. It will take me a little time to find a job and a place to live."

"I'll look for what's available in Rawhide," Harry said. "Maybe my old apartment over the sheriff's office."

John shook his head. "No, that's rented. Besides, it only has one bedroom. Emma wouldn't sleep well without her own room. You should see the one Mom made here."

"The baby has her own room? Is she in my room?" Melissa asked.

"No, I'm afraid I'm in your room, Melissa. But Camille made a special room next door. Would you like to come see it?" Lucy offered.

"Yes, I would. Will we wake up the baby?"

"She's due up at eight, and it's almost that time now."

"I'll come along, Lucy, if you don't mind," Harry said. "I'd like to meet my only niece."

Camille began clearing the table as those three left the room. John wanted to go with them, but he couldn't abandon his mother with all the work. Griff got up to help, also, and they quickly cleared the table.

Then John headed for Emma's room, anxious to see how the meeting had gone.

When he reached the door to Emma's room, he came face-to-face with Harry, carrying Emma.

"Look, John, isn't she great?"

"Yeah, she looks like her mama," John said with a smile.

"She does, doesn't she? I didn't meet Cecil but once or twice, but I really didn't like him much. I'm glad Emma looks like Lucy."

"Me, too."

Emma reached out for John. "Ah, come here, baby girl. I'll carry you."

"Hey, no fair. You've had six weeks with her," Harry protested, but he gave Emma up to John.

"She's a little partial to John," Lucy said softly.

"Yeah, I can tell," Harry said with a grin.

"I really like this room, Lucy. When you move out, I hope Mom will keep the room for when Emma visits and when my baby comes to visit."

"Yes, I'm sure she will. I need to fix Emma's bottle."

"Of course."

When they reached the kitchen, they discovered Camille had already fixed Emma's bottle.

"Oh, thank you, Camille," Lucy said, taking the bottle. But John took it from her and sat down at the table to feed Emma.

Lucy settled in the chair beside him, in case her baby needed her.

"I suppose Dad is the only one who hasn't fed her," Melissa said.

"Not true. I fed her her first day home from the hospital," Griff said. "She loved it."

"She always loves her bottle," John said. "I fed her that first bottle while Lucy slept."

"Was the childbirth difficult?" Melissa asked, concern in her gaze.

"No, not really. Caro gives good drugs," Lucy told Melissa.

"I know she's a good doctor, but thanks for telling me that," Melissa said, smiling warmly at Lucy.

"Of course, she was only in labor for about half an hour," John added.

Melissa's eyes grew large.

Before she could say anything, Lucy said, "That's because I was in labor off and on during the night before I got to the hospital."

"Oh. That must've been difficult for you."

"Yes, it was, but John... I mean, I got to the hospital in plenty of time." Lucy smiled at Melissa.

"I guess it's been a long journey for you."

"Yes, but your journey will be much nicer. I hope Harry is being a good husband."

"He's the best," Melissa said with a big smile for her husband.

Camille sent a big smile to Harry, also. "I knew he'd be a good husband."

"Thanks, Camille," Harry said.

"Now, when is your baby due?"

"We're not sure. She's going to go see Caro next week. She'll help us with the details."

"I think they do a sonogram early these days," Camille said. "Will you call us with the date?"

"Of course. But I think we'd better head for home. Melissa still has to catch up on her sleep."

They all said their goodbyes, even John. Emma looked at them leaving but didn't stop taking her bottle.

"Really, Emma," Camille teased, "at least you could take a breath."

"I'm afraid she's hungry. Of course, her uncle John encouraged her to keep eating," Griff pointed out. "If only he'd taken the bottle out of her mouth for thirty seconds!"

John immediately did so. "You want to see what she'd do?" John asked. "What do you think, Emma, my love?"

Emma began cooing to John.

"That's right, sweetheart. I knew you would be a good girl."

Lucy stepped forward. "Maybe I'd better finish giving her the bottle. You're too distracting, John."

"To Emma or to you, Lucy?" John asked, winking at her.

AT BREAKFAST the next morning, Griff asked Lucy, "Have you figured out anything that you want to do?"

"I took a lot of accounting courses. Is there an accounting office in Rawhide?"

Camille was eating some scrambled eggs, but she almost choked at that question. When she could speak again, she said, "You met Tori, didn't you? Brett and Anna's daughter?"

"No. I don't think so."

"She and her cousin Russ own the accounting firm in town and she does the investing for a lot of the family, conferring with Griff, of course."

Lucy stared at Camille. "Really?"

"Yes, dear, I'm sorry, I thought you knew."

"She met a lot of Randalls that first week," Griff said.

"So if I wanted to work for them, they might try me out? If they needed someone."

"Just happens they do. And I guess I could recommend you," he said with a grin.

"But you don't know whether I'm any good or not, Griff," Lucy protested. "I can't ask you to do that."

"Hmm, maybe I could give you a test? How much is twelve times twelve?"

Lucy laughed with him. "All I'm asking, Griff, is a fair chance to take a test and see if they would give me a chance."

"Okay, how about we go into town this morning. You can talk to Russ and Tori."

"Today?" Lucy asked. Then she gulped. "Okay. Can we be back in time to feed Emma?"

"I can feed Emma," Camille said. "I'd be happy to. It's been hard for me to get a chance to hold her when John's around."

"Okay. I guess we could go. I have to get ready. I'm not sure I have anything to wear."

"I think I can loan you a few things." Camille got up from the table. "Let me go lay out a couple of things for you to borrow."

"I should—" Lucy began, but Emma still had to finish her bottle.

"Hand me the little girl. I don't need to look at clothes. The two of us will be right here when you finish," Griff said, leaning over to take Emma from Lucy.

"Thank you, Griff. I'll hurry."

LUCY, DRESSED IN her own black pants and Camille's black shirt and herringbone jacket, looked and felt good when she got to the accounting office. She was accompanied by Griff.

"Are you sure this is a good idea?" Lucy whispered as he opened the door for her.

"I'm sure."

"Hi, Griff," Tori greeted him. "Hello," she said to Lucy.

"This is Lucy, Harry's sister. She's staying with us."

"Welcome. I was getting a cup of coffee. I needed a break. Can I interest either or both of you in some?"

"I'll take a cup. How about you, Lucy?"

"Uh, no, Griff, I mean, Tori. Thanks anyway. I'm here to talk to you about possibly working for you and Russ."

Tori's eyes lit up. "You're looking for a job? Do you have any accounting training?"

"I don't have any work experience, but I took some accounting in college."

"Oh, really? Do you mind taking a test?"

"No, of course not."

"All right. Let me talk to Russ and pull something together. Will you excuse me?"

Lucy nodded, still standing near the front door.

"Come on, Lucy, sit down," Griff ordered. "You can't stand at attention while they're making up a test for you."

"But what if I can't do it, Griff?"

"Lucy, you gotta believe. What if you get the job? Then you have to go tell Camille and John. That could be tougher than the test."

Lucy sat down next to Griff. "I owe you for bringing me down. I would've put it off if you hadn't forced me to come this morning."

"I know. But if you'd worried about it for several

days, I figured you would've gotten cold feet. Now, it'll be over in an hour or two."

Russ's door opened and he came out with Tori. "Lucy, I'm glad to meet you."

"Yes, I'm glad to meet you, too. I'm here looking for a job."

"Yes, that's what Tori said. We need some help right now, and we'd be glad to take you on if your skills are reasonable."

"I hope so, too. Do you have a test I can take?"

"It just so happens we do. If you'll sit at that desk, there are pencils in the drawer."

Lucy moved to the desk, trying to swallow past a suddenly dry throat and casting a look at Griff. Once seated, she looked at Russ. "I'm ready."

He handed her a page of figures. "You're going to be timed."

"Yes. Thank you."

Russ came over to greet Griff quietly as Lucy worked away in the background.

"I can't tell you how much we want this to work," Russ said.

"Me, too. Lucy needs to feel good about herself." Griff grinned at Russ. "Of course, she'll have to figure what to do with her baby if she gets the job."

"Hmm, we could work something out. I'm telling you we're desperate. We're falling behind since Bill passed away."

"Yeah. That was sad."

"I'm finished." Lucy stood at the desk, holding out the paper they had given her.

Tori took it. "Thanks, Lucy." She looked at it and then handed it to Russ.

"Excellent, Lucy. You would be welcome here. As soon as possible, actually. Will you come work with us?"

"I have to find a place to live and somewhere to leave my baby."

"Why don't you bring your baby to work with you?" Tori asked. "I did that when mine were little."

"Seriously?" Lucy asked, staring at Tori.

"Oh, yes. We can do that until your baby starts getting noisy."

"That would be wonderful. Now, if I can only find a place to live."

"I can help there," Russ said. "One of the upstairs apartments is vacant. It has two bedrooms, two baths, a living area with a fireplace and a nice kitchen and breakfast area. You want to see it?"

"Yes, please."

Griff and Tori followed the pair leaving the office.

"I haven't seen one of the apartments since Russ lived in it before he married Isabella. Have they changed much?"

"No. Actually, this one has a lot of furniture. A deputy came in to town and moved in with no furniture. Half the family volunteered leftovers. I'd bet Russ is hoping she'll need some furniture so he won't have to move it out."

"Is there a crib?"

"No, I'm afraid not."

"We might be able to buy a crib for Emma."

"I'm glad the baby was born healthy. It wasn't a very happy start, but I heard John helped her out with his sharpshooting."

"Yeah. He wasn't sure he wanted to do that, but he wouldn't trust it to anyone else."

"Well, Lucy seems to have come through very well."

"Yeah, she's one fine little lady."

Chapter Twelve

Lucy sat silently in the truck next to Griff, afraid to speak. She might bubble over if she tried to talk.

"You're being awfully quiet, Lucy. I hope you're happy about everything," Griff said after a few minutes.

"Oh, I'm ecstatic! I'm afraid if I start talking I won't be able to stop. I've never had a job of my own, or a place to live that I'm paying for. See what I mean?"

Griff smiled. "I see. Well, you'd better save your enthusiasm because you're going to have to make Camille happy now."

"Oh, I think that'll be easy. To be in charge of my life is so amazing. I never was the decision maker. I know I'll make mistakes, but I can make choices!"

Griff actually chuckled. "You think life is going to be good?"

"I think it'll be incredible!"

Griff parked the truck beside the house and they both went inside.

Camille jumped up. "How did the interview go?"

"It was amazing," Lucy gushed. "They liked me,

they liked my skills and they say it's fine for me to bring Emma to the office!"

"Bringing Emma to the office? Why would you do that?" Camille asked sharply.

Lucy shared a look with Griff. "Because she's very quiet and there's no one there for her to bother. Both Russ and Tori can close their doors if she's a bother. Just for a few months. When she gets older, I'll have to find a sitter."

"I think she should stay here with me. She'll be able to sleep in her own crib! That would be better."

"But—but I won't be living here. Russ has a really neat apartment upstairs, with two bedrooms. I'll be a few feet from my apartment when I go to work."

"But I want you to stay here!" Camille said.

Griff walked over and put his arm around his wife. "Little birds grow up and have to try their wings."

"But, Griff, she needs me to help her with the baby and do her laundry. She can't manage on her own," Camille protested.

"That's the other nice thing, Camille. The apartment has a washer and dryer. I can do my own laundry right there in the apartment."

"But you'll be tired, after working all day. I can have dinner on the table and several loads of clothes done when you come in the door."

"But you should be enjoying your life, not doing my chores. You've got a grandchild coming. You may want to make things for Melissa's baby."

Camille turned her body into Griff's and hid her face on his chest.

Lucy knew she was crying, but she didn't know what to say. Finally, she patted Camille on the shoulder. "Camille, you've done so much for me. I'll do whatever you want me to do. Right now I'm going to go check on Emma."

Once Lucy had left the room, Griff eased Camille away from him a little. "I have to tell you how excited Lucy was on the way home. She's never lived alone, held down a job, made decisions, except when she made the wise choice to leave Cecil. She was like a different woman, filled with courage to do all these things on her own."

Camille sniffed. "She might've left him earlier if she'd known how to live her own life. You're telling me I need to let her do that."

"Do you remember how you told me Melissa deserved the chance to learn how to live while we were still here to help her? Lucy needs to make her decisions for the first time with us nearby. But she needs to make them."

"Yes, but—but will she come back to us? It took Melissa six years before she came back."

"I know, sweetheart, but you were the most patient mother anyone could have. Lucy didn't have a mother who loved her daughter enough to sacrifice for her. But you can be that mother for Lucy. You can stand back and let her make her decisions and answer any questions she has. And welcome her back home whenever she wants to come."

"John's not going to be happy, either," Camille said, her chin signaling her stubbornness.

"I know. But he's going to have to let her have her independence, too. I'll talk to him before he comes in for dinner."

Lucy came back into the room with Emma in her arms. "Look, Emma is awake. She wasn't crying, though."

"Hello, Emma, my girl. Did Mama tell you what a great morning she had?" Griff asked the baby.

"I told her about everything. Camille, have you thought about my job and my place to live?"

"Yes, Lucy," Camille said, hugging her. "I don't like it, but I realize you need to spread your wings. But you must promise to ask for help or ask questions if you need to. Or borrow money if you run short, as if we were your parents. Will you promise to do that?"

"Of course, Camille. What a wonderful offer. But I'll try not to bother you too much. I would like to come visit every once in a while."

"Of course. We expect that. If we don't see Emma often enough, we might not recognize her."

"You'll see her as often as you like. And if you come to town, you can stop in the office and visit."

"Good deal," Camille said. "When do you start?"

GRIFF WAS IN the horse barn waiting for his son when John rode in. He was tired. He'd worked long and hard, moving a herd to a nearer pasture for the winter.

"Hi, Dad. What's up?"

"Not much. I, uh, took Lucy to see Russ and Tori today."

"Why?"

"It turns out that Lucy does accounting. She's never actually had a job, but that's what she'd studied in college."

John had been unsaddling his horse as his father talked. When he reached the end of his explanation, John swung around, with the saddle in his hands and said, "Are you telling me that they gave her a job, just like that?"

"And an apartment, too. She can even bring Emma to the office while she works. Everything's set up."

"Dad, what did you do? Lucy's never lived on her own."

"That's the point. Lucy is so excited about living in her own place, just her and Emma. She may hate it after a while. It may be too much for her. But she has the right to try. She gets to make decisions that are good for her and Emma. And if she gets in trouble, we can be there to lend a hand."

"Damn it, Dad, that's not what I want! I want to help take care of Emma. I want to protect Lucy so she won't be hurt again! I want—"

"I know you're in love with Lucy. But do you think she's ready for another relationship? Do you think she'll want to make a family with you? If she does, she'll realize it a lot faster going out on her own."

"But Emma is so little."

"Of course she is. But she'll also keep Lucy from having a social life. That's a good thing, don't you think?"

"Well, yeah, I guess."

"Lucy is going to be careful. Just keep that in mind."

"Of course, but— Okay, I'll be happy for her. That's what you're telling me, isn't it?"

"Yeah. And be positive with your mom, too. She's having a hard time letting go of Lucy and that sweet baby."

"You're sure this is going to be all right?"

"I think it's the only way it will be all right."

LUCY AND EMMA MOVED into the apartment in Rawhide the next Sunday. Camille, Griff and John helped Lucy gather her and Emma's belongings and move them to the apartment. Camille and Griff bought a new crib.

Once they set it up, Lucy was thrilled with the way the room looked for her child. Her own room looked wonderful, too, thanks to the bedding Camille brought.

"I can't thank you enough, Camille."

"I want you to have a comfortable place to rest. Griff bought you a television this afternoon, too. He's bringing it up now. That way you can watch your favorite shows in the evenings."

"And I bought you this," John announced from the hallway, holding a wooden rocker. "Where do you want this?"

"Oh, it's beautiful, John. I hadn't thought about not having a rocker for Emma. Thank you so much," Lucy said, putting her arms around John's neck after he set the rocker down in the living room.

John put his arms around Lucy and held her tightly. Then he set her loose and suggested she put it exactly where she wanted it. Lucy looked around the room and chose the space near the breakfast nook but still near the television that Griff was now setting up.

"I have everything I need! It's wonderful, thanks to you three. I can't thank you enough," she said again.

"No, you don't have everything you need. I'm taking you grocery shopping. John will go with us so he can carry your groceries once we buy them."

"But, Camille, I can buy my own groceries," Lucy protested.

"Not your first groceries, dear. That's what I can do. Then, I promise, I'll let you manage on your own."

Lucy hugged Camille. "You are so sweet to me, Camille. Thank you."

The three of them went shopping. Camille was buying a lot of things for Lucy that she didn't think she really needed. After they checked out, John carried the sacks.

"You'll have to get John to come grocery shopping with you next time, Lucy, or you won't be able to get your purchases home. He's very handy to have around."

"He is certainly being helpful today. All of you are."

"With good reason. We expect you to do well. And we're going to be here to help you."

When the day had come to an end, and Emma was sleeping in her new bed and Lucy was ready for hers, too, the three Randalls were ready to leave. Camille gave Lucy a hug and reminded her to call if she needed anything. Griff gave Lucy a hug and said, "We're only a phone call away."

John was the last to leave. He lingered at her doorway after his parents had gone. "I'll check on you and Emma as often as I can."

Lucy smiled at him. "I know you will, John. I—"

But she never got to finish, as John swooped down and captured her lips. Just as quickly he was gone.

Lucy realized then how much she'd miss him.

LUCY SETTLED into a routine. She got up at eight with Emma, gave her her bottle and dressed her. Then she ate some oatmeal and dressed for work. Then, with Emma in tow, Lucy descended the steps and arrived at work at nine o'clock.

She'd bought a baby carrier that acted as a rocker. Emma loved being rocked back and forth as she curled up and went to sleep. When she woke up at noon, Lucy would take her upstairs and fix her a new bottle, change her diaper and rock her to sleep.

When lunch was over, she'd return to the office, with Emma sleeping soundly beside her, and finish her workday.

At first, she didn't see any of the three Randalls. Then John came in at lunch one day and ate with her. He fed Emma while she fixed their meal. It was a lovely diversion from her normal routine.

John came one evening, bringing some cookies his mom had baked.

Lucy offered to fix dinner for the two of them, after Emma went to bed.

"I didn't come to make extra work for you, Lucy," John said.

"It would be fun to eat with someone, instead of always eating alone. I didn't realize how much I'd miss being with all of you."

"We miss you, too. And we miss Emma," John said, cuddling the baby against him.

Emma started cooing, reaching for his face.

"You're the only one she ever coos at besides me. She just loves your voice."

"And I love her."

"That makes her a lucky little girl. If her father had lived, I don't know—"

"You're the one who made the difference there. You left after he beat you. You got away and had your baby here."

"With you."

"I wanted to be there for you."

"You were. You were wonderful to both of us."

"The three of us share that time."

"Yes, we do. I don't know how we'll explain the connection if you ever get married. Your wife wouldn't appreciate Emma and I hanging around." And she would have to move away if that happened.

"Maybe you'll be the one to marry first."

Lucy looked away. "I don't think so."

"Why not?"

"I'm —I'm no good at marriage."

"It takes two to make a marriage. And I don't think you had a good partner."

"I think I was partly at fault. I didn't— He didn't— Never mind. Let's change the subject."

"All right. Your daughter is finished with her bottle. Do you want me to put her down, or leave her up for a little while?"

"Oh, I think she'll like talking to you. I want her to know a good man."

"You understand she's not going to believe you if you don't have anything to do with a man, don't you?"

"I'll worry about that when she's older."

"What do you say about that, Emma?" John asked the baby. Emma cooed a lot, enjoying his voice. He bent down to kiss her rosy cheek.

John looked up suddenly, feeling Lucy's stare. "What is it, Lucy?"

"Nothing! Nothing at all. Are you ready to eat? I think dinner's ready." It had suddenly struck her how much she and Emma would miss John if they had to leave.

"Sure. Is it okay for me to hold Emma while I eat?"

"Yes, of course. Or I can hold her."

"I've missed her. I'll hold her and we can talk to her while we eat. It smells good."

"It's a casserole your mom taught me to make."

"Ah, I thought I recognized it. I enjoy casseroles."

"I'm going to buy a Crock-Pot and learn to cook with it. I can start dinner in the morning."

"That's a good idea. It makes me want to drop by and taste what you're cooking."

"You're welcome anytime. Is your mom doing all right?"

"She misses you. She's been cooking up a storm. She usually does that when she's worried about something."

"I'll come out on Saturday for lunch, if you can tell her I'll be there."

"I'll do that. It should make her happy."

After they ate, John got up to go.

"Thank you for coming, John. I hope you'll come back."

"How about Saturday night, after your visit with Mom and Dad?"

"All right. I'll plan a dinner and cook it in the new Crock-Pot I'm going to buy."

"Good." He suddenly bent down and kissed her lips. "I'll see you Saturday."

Then he walked out.

Lucy stood there, holding on to the door. You'd think she'd expect a kiss from John by now, but it still surprised her. She reached up to feel her lips. It was a kiss so totally different from what she'd experienced with her husband.

Totally different.

SATURDAY WAS A BIG DAY for Lucy. She packed up her baby and diapers, changes of clothes and bottles for the day and drove to the Randall ranch, arriving about ten o'clock. It had been two weeks of working, a new experience for Lucy.

She was eager to see Camille again. She'd talked to her several times, but she couldn't wait to hug her and tell her all about her work.

When Lucy entered with Emma, John surprised her by being at home. He reached for the baby.

"John Randall, that is not fair!" Camille exclaimed.

John immediately surrendered the baby to Camille, who also took time to hug Lucy.

"Are we too early? I was excited to come see you, Camille. If we're too early—"

"Nonsense, child. You're exactly on time, whenever you come."

"Thank you, Camille. Emma is staying awake longer. I put off her bottle, but it's time for another one."

Lucy took out a bottle already prepared. "Would you like to feed her, Camille?"

"I'd love to."

Lucy handed over the bottle.

"Good, now I'll take Lucy to the barn to see the new foal we had today." John took Lucy's arm and headed for the barn.

"But I was going to visit with your mom."

"Hey, she gets to feed Emma. So I get you. Besides, you'll have time to visit over lunch when she won't be playing with Emma."

"Oh, all right. You have a foal? Isn't it the wrong time of the year?"

"Well, maybe he's not newborn. But we had to bring him in because he was in an accident with a fence. He's a handsome fellow, though. You'll see," John said with a grin as he held open the barn door.

"I didn't visit the barn when I lived here. I guess that was because of Emma. She's not as demanding as she was those first weeks."

"Good, because you have a lot less time with this job. How's it going, by the way?"

"Just fine. It makes me feel good to be able to hold down a job. Cecil used to say— Never mind. I'm not going to think about him or what he said."

"Good. Here's the little guy. He's almost grown. Just a few more months to his first birthday. I was thinking about giving him to Emma."

"But Emma isn't even two months old. And she has no place to keep a horse. Besides, I wouldn't know how to take care of a horse!"

"I thought I'd keep him here for when Emma starts riding."

"And when do you think that will happen?"

"Around three. I can take her up on my horse until then."

"John Randall, you're being ridiculous! I wouldn't let Emma on a horse no matter who's riding with her."

"But you know she'd come ride with me. We'd be careful!"

"No. Not that young."

"Okay, how about you start riding. Then we'll discuss Emma's debut later."

Chapter Thirteen

Lucy enjoyed lunch with the Randalls. Griff asked about her job and how she was adjusting to the office. Camille laughed at her stories of Emma, while John seemed interested in her few visits from Harry, which had gone well.

"It's going to take a while to get used to, but I'm glad to have my brother back in my life. I told him I'd save Emma's clothes in case they have a girl."

"That would be nice," Camille said. "It's amazing how quickly she's grown."

Lucy nodded. "Sometimes I want to tell her to stop growing, but I know it's healthy. We go back to Caro for her checkup next week."

"When do you go?" John asked.

Lucy had tried to avoid looking at John since they'd come back from the barn. She'd even made sure she didn't sit next to him. Now, though, she briefly met his eyes and felt her body come alive. She nearly forgot his question. "Tuesday morning at eight-thirty."

"That's early."

"We can manage. I'll have to wake Emma up and get her started early."

"Won't Tori and Russ give you time off?" Griff asked.

"They would, but we're still behind, though I've worked as hard as I can," Lucy said, a frown on her face. "I don't want to ask for time off."

"Do you work until five?" John asked.

"No, I finish at four. Sometimes I work a little longer when Emma sleeps past four, but not often. She usually is ready for a bottle at four."

"I remember," John said with a smile.

Lucy remembered, too, the time he'd spent with Emma…and with her, especially late at night when the house was dark and silent. She looked down at her plate.

"I could come pick Emma up after her noon bottle and bring her back here for the afternoon on, say, Wednesday, and you could work until six and join us here for dinner and pick up Emma."

"Oh, Camille, I can't ask you to do that."

"I'd love it. I don't want to forget how to take care of a baby. Melissa will be needing help, too, you know."

"Harry said they were looking for a housekeeper. He offered me the job, but I told him I was happy where I was." Lucy bit her bottom lip. "I felt a little mean telling him no. I know he needs good help."

"Well, it was nice of him to think of you, but your skills are valuable." Griff smiled at her.

"Thank you. Tori said the same thing, which was nice of her."

"Nice?" Griff snorted. "She'd fight for your services! I heard her telling someone at lunch what a savior you'd been, taking some of the pressure off both her and Russ."

"That's really kind. But I'm not nearly as skilled as either of them. I have a lot to learn."

"That's expected, but you're coming along quickly," Griff told her.

Lucy smiled at him. He made her feel so much better.

"So how do you fill your off time?" John asked.

Lucy looked at him blankly. "My off time? What's that? I occasionally watch a TV show, but after I take care of Emma, I have to do laundry and clean the house."

"I see. Will my coming over this evening disrupt you?" John asked.

Lucy hadn't been sure he was coming, but she'd gotten up early to tidy her apartment, just in case. But now, after his remarks in the barn, she wasn't sure it was a good idea. Still, she couldn't lie to him. "No, it'll be fine."

"Good."

"I didn't know you were going to Lucy's tonight. Did you, Griff?" Camille asked.

"Nope. None of my business, as long as Lucy's not protesting."

"No, of course not," Lucy said, feeling John's gaze on her. "I lo— Emma loves to see him."

"That's right. She's my girl." He grinned at Lucy.

She could almost hear his unspoken words. *And so are you.*

WHEN LUCY PACKED UP to go home, she found John there to lend a hand.

"Don't you have to work today?" she asked.

"Nope. I took the time off. Is Emma asleep?"

"Yes, she stayed asleep when I put her in her car seat."

"Okay. Will she wake up when we get her home?"

"I'm not sure. She usually sleeps until four o'clock. Maybe later because she stayed awake with your mom."

"We can visit while she sleeps."

"Y-yes, I guess so."

John just smiled, which made Lucy worry about what he had in mind. At least there were no horses in her apartment. He couldn't start teaching her how to ride there.

When they reached her apartment, Lucy felt proud of her place. She'd bought a few things, but everything was scrubbed and put away. When Emma got older, it would be harder to keep the apartment straight, but today, she'd done her job.

"The place looks good, Lucy. You must've worked hard."

"I lived in your mom's house. I want to keep up with her standards."

"She is good, isn't she?" John asked with a grin.

"Yes, she is. And I want Emma to learn from me. It's important."

"Yeah, but you can't work all the time. You've got to play some, too."

"Does your mother play?"

"Yeah, she does. She sees her friends and reads a lot in her spare time."

Lucy felt uncomfortable in the apartment alone with John. She wished Emma would awaken to break the ice. "Why don't we turn on the television? I think football is on today."

"It always is on Saturdays."

John turned on the television and found the game he wanted to watch. When they sat on the sofa—too close for Lucy's comfort—he started explaining the game to her. She was able to follow most of his explanations.

"You know an awful lot about football," she said. "If you ever got where you couldn't be a cowboy, you could make a living explaining football."

"Hmm, I'll have to think about that. It might be easier than being a cowboy."

"I think it must be painful to ride a horse for so long every day."

"Just in the beginning. You train your muscles. It won't take you long."

"Does Camille ride?"

"Yeah, but not often."

"Well, as long as I live here, I don't see any need to ride."

"But what if you move back out to the ranch?"

Lucy stared at John. "Why would I do that?"

"What if we got married?"

Lucy felt as if she'd been hit in the stomach by a prizefighter. All the air went out of her. "I don't know what you're talking about."

"I'm talking about us getting married. Don't you think that's a good idea?"

"No! No, I don't! I told you I won't be getting married. That's not me."

"Getting married's not you? Why not?"

"My marriage was not good. Why would I want to try again?"

"Because marriage can be wonderful. Just because you messed up once doesn't mean you don't want to try again."

She waved him off with her hand. "I don't want to talk about this. Let's go back to football." At least then she'd be able to breathe.

But John was persistent. "I think we should talk about marriage. What did you dislike about it?"

"Everything," Lucy said in clipped tones.

John put his arm on the back of the sofa and Lucy shifted away a foot. "Intimacy? Did you hate that?"

"Yes."

"Surely you did some cuddling before you got married."

She swallowed hard. "Very little."

"How long did you date?"

"About six months."

"Man, he must've really been slow."

"What do you mean?"

"Lucy, if you were my girl, I'd do all the cuddling you'd allow."

Despite her rapidly accelerating pulse she snapped, "Maybe I wouldn't allow any."

"Surely you'd allow a kiss or two…like this?" he

asked, leaning over and kissing her gently. "That wasn't too bad, was it?"

Bad? It was heaven. "No, but—but we're not dating." She was desparate for a reason they should stop, but that sounded lame even to her.

"We aren't? Are you sure?"

"Yes, we're just…friends."

"Right," he agreed, and leaned over and kissed her again.

She pulled back and put a palm on his chest. Big mistake. It was rock-hard and she'd love to explore it.

"You must stop that."

"Why? Isn't it fun?"

"It's not something we should be doing."

"Didn't you kiss anyone other than your husband?"

"After we were married?" Lucy asked, horrified.

"No, before. Didn't you date other people?"

"Not really."

"Then you need to play around now. Find out what it's all about." He kissed her again, this time more deeply.

When he moved back, she was breathing heavily. "I don't…think we need to do that."

"It's the only way you'll learn about love, Lucy. You can't just read about it, or hear about it or dream about it. You have to try it." He let his arm settle on her shoulders and pull her closer. He kissed her again, this time his tongue entering her mouth.

She jerked away. "No!"

"Easy, Lucy. It's all right."

"No, I can't—"

"Shh, Lucy. Just relax. Let's just sit here for a minute."

"Why did you do that?"

"It's called French-kissing. Did you ever do that with your husband?"

"No. We didn't k-kiss much."

"Damn, that's terrible. Kissing is great. You need to practice a lot." He immediately initiated more kissing. This time, he could feel a difference. She'd stopped fighting him, and relaxed against him.

After about half an hour, John pulled back. "Okay, I think that's enough of a lesson tonight. How about supper?"

"Did I do something wrong?" Lucy asked.

"Oh, no, honey, but a guy can only go so far before he wants to take it to a higher level, and I'm not sure you're ready for that."

"I see."

"Do you want me to help fix supper? I'm pretty good in the kitchen."

"No. I've got it all ready. I'll just set the table," she said, jumping up from the sofa.

She began setting the table. Then she heated up some green beans in the microwave. Finally, she unplugged the Crock-Pot. Taking the lid off, she emptied the contents into a casserole dish.

"That smells good," he said, coming up behind her.

"Thank you," Lucy said, sidestepping him to grab some condiments. "Dinner is ready."

John joined her at the table and she passed him the dishes. He filled his plate and ate well. "You're a good cook, Lucy."

"That's a real compliment since you eat Camille's cooking every day."

"You're just as good a cook."

When he'd finished his meal, Lucy cleared away the dishes and warmed up the apple cobbler she'd made earlier. She served it with vanilla ice cream.

"This is wonderful, Lucy."

"Thank you."

After they ate, they did the dishes together.

"This is nice, sharing the chores," John told her with a smile.

"Yes, it is. You're very good at cleaning up."

"It's a Randall tradition. In this family, everyone helps with the cleanup. When it was just the four brothers, Red was the cook, and he insisted they all know how to cook and how to clean up. It's still the tradition. Dad and I help Mom clean up after dinner. After all, she did all the cooking because we were working."

"I like that about you and your dad."

"Did your husband help clean up?"

"No. But I didn't mind. He was always drunk by the end of dinner. All he did was sit in his chair and drink."

"That sounds terrible. No wonder you're soured on marriage. Didn't you share anything?"

"No." Her tones were clipped again, as they got when she didn't want to talk.

"Say, have you met Russ and Isabella's children?"

"No. Isabella came to the office one day, but I haven't seen her or the children since."

"You'd laugh if you saw the kids. The little girl takes

after her mother. They call her Angel. She was about Emma's size when Russ found her and her mother on the side of the road in a snowstorm. He took them to Rawhide but had to take them into his apartment, this very one you live in. Russ had lost his first wife when she was pregnant."

"I didn't know that!"

"It's not something he talks about. When he found Izzy and Angel, he refused to have anything to do with little children. But he had to take them in because of the storm. Izzy was sick and he had to take care of Angel. By the time Izzy was well, Russ was in love with Angel." He smiled broadly. "She's the happiest child you've ever seen."

"Does she look like Isabella, because she's certainly beautiful."

"Yeah, she does. But their little boy is all Russ. You know he's a twin?"

"Russ is a twin? Who's his brother?"

"Well, he has two brothers, but Rich is his twin. He's Samantha's husband."

"I haven't met her."

"Yeah. She rescued Rich from a broken ankle, driving him home, not knowing that she already knew his father."

"How could she not know?"

"She didn't know Pete's last name. She was cleaning the stables at the rodeos with her dad when she was little. Pete was a sucker for a kid in trouble. He tried to adopt her, but her dad wouldn't turn her loose. Instead, he packed up and moved on. After her father died when she was sixteen, she continued to work the rodeos, but she had problems with the randy cowboys and switched to waitressing."

"Sounds like she had a rough life."

"Yeah, and it took a while to get it straightened out. But the Randalls are lucky in love."

"Are you?"

"Yeah, I think I am. I've been wanting to marry and have a family, but I've refused to consider it until I felt the way Dad does about Mom."

"Yes, I can see how that would affect you. But maybe you'll get lucky like the others and suddenly find the woman for you."

A curious smile played about his lips as he said, "Oh, it's happened for me, too. I finally met the woman of my dreams."

"I see. Well, I wish you the best, John. You deserve it." She knew she was saying the right thing, but she was trembling inside, afraid the time had come for John to leave.

"Thank you. I think I do, too."

"When will you be marrying? Have I met her yet?"

"I think so. You see, I met her one night on a lonely road. She was stranded and so was I. We spent the night together. Holding her in my arms, I knew she was the one for me."

"John, that sounds like— I mean, you can't mean me?"

"Why not?"

"I think you have terrible luck."

"I don't." He scooted forward. "Kiss me, Lucy." She

hesitated, but he pulled her back into his arms for a kiss. "Yeah, it's definitely you," he said when he released her.

"How can you tell?"

"Because I'd rather be here with you, doing nothing, then anywhere in the world with anyone else."

"Oh, John, I don't think you're lucky in love."

"Oh, yeah, I'm definitely lucky. You just wait and see."

"I don't think you should tell your parents how you feel."

John laughed. "They already know, honey. Dad has told me I shouldn't rush you."

"I don't think you're taking his advice."

John pulled her close again, her breasts against his chest. "I'm trying, Lucy. Trust me, I am."

Chapter Fourteen

On Tuesday morning, Lucy was almost ready to leave for the doctor's when a knock sounded on her door.

Surprised, she peered out the peephole and saw John standing there. She hurriedly opened the door. "John, what are you doing here?"

"I've come to take you to the doctor's office."

"Aren't you riding out today?"

"Nope. It's time for your appointment. I don't want you to go alone."

"It's not anything big, John. We're just getting a checkup."

"I know. Just think of it as an extension of delivery. Are you ready?"

"I was just giving Emma some of her bottle. Not all. I don't want her to fall asleep."

"Aha. Let me talk to her."

John stepped into the apartment and walked to the table where Emma's carrier sat. "Good morning, Emma, my love. How are you?"

As if on cue, Emma cooed to John, obviously happy to see him.

"Okay! I guess that means we're ready to go. Will you carry her?"

"Of course. My truck is right by the stairs. We'll be there in two seconds."

After donning her coat, and making sure Emma was well wrapped in her blanket, Lucy opened the door and stepped out into the cold air. "Did a front come through? It's cold out here!"

"Yeah. That's why I'm parked by the stairs. That's the closest I could get."

"I guess I shouldn't be surprised since it's the beginning of December. Even in Kansas City we might have snow by now."

"Yeah," John agreed. They reached the bottom of the stairs and his truck. He opened the passenger door for Lucy and handed in Emma.

When he got behind the wheel, he immediately put his truck in gear and started toward the clinic. The heater was already warmed up and blew hot air into the cab.

"You left the motor running? Weren't you worried about someone stealing it?"

"In Rawhide?" John asked with a laugh. "Usually you have to have strangers around for things like that to happen. In Rawhide, we don't have strangers very often. If we do, they stand out like a sore thumb."

As John had said, they were at the clinic almost immediately. Lucy managed to get Emma's carrier out and started up the steps as John joined her.

"Hey, Emma, are you doing okay?" John asked the baby. She again responded with her coos.

"You know, Lucy, I think Emma will start talking soon. She's trying so hard."

"Sometimes I think so, too. But then she never actually says words. Not even *Mama*."

"I think she says *Dada* sometimes."

Lucy gave him a strange look. But a nurse met them as they entered and she didn't say anything about his comment.

"Dr. Randall is waiting for you. If you'll come with me," she said, and led the way down the hall to an examination room. "You'll need to undress the baby."

Lucy took Emma out of the carrier and began to take off her sleeper. "You be a good girl, Emma, so the doctor can examine you."

John leaned over, resting his elbows on the examining table to talk to Emma. "Of course, she'll be good, right, Emma?"

Once again Emma tried to talk to the man who Lucy perceived as her favorite person. It sometimes made her a little jealous that Emma responded to John that way.

Just then, the door opened and Caroline came in.

"Good morning, Lucy. Hi, John. I didn't know you'd be here."

"I like to be at everything important for Emma. She's my girl!"

Again the baby cooed at him.

"Well, she certainly seems in agreement. Hello, Emma, are you ready to be examined?"

"I left her diaper on until you were ready," Lucy said. "I didn't want to mess up your room."

"Thanks, Lucy. How is she doing? Any problems?"

"She's doing great. She's sleeping four hours between bottles and she wakes up happy. She only cries when she wants my attention, mostly to wake me up."

"Very good." Caroline measured her. "She's growing nicely." Then she gave her a complete examination. "Very nice, Lucy. You're doing a good job."

"Thank you," Lucy said.

"Now, the only thing is to draw her blood. She's going to cry. Are you prepared for that?"

Lucy swallowed and nodded. John, however, hadn't realized they would do that. "Is that really necessary?"

"Yes, John, it is. You can hold her if you want."

John looked at Lucy. "Yes, I'll hold her."

Emma cried as predicted. Lucy tried to soothe her with soft touches and an even softer voice, while John held her close.

"Come to Mama, baby girl," Lucy said, taking Emma in her arms and offering her her bottle. Emma began sucking her bottle and Lucy gently wiped away the tears that filled her own eyes. "Will there be anything else?"

"No, Lucy. You did fine with Emma. She'll have to take some shots in a few months, though. So you'll have to be prepared."

"Okay," Lucy agreed, holding back tears.

"Now, once Emma is dressed, let John take her to the waiting room and we'll do your checkup. We should've done it at six weeks." Caroline smiled at all three of them and left the room.

Lucy dressed her baby, continuing to soothe her, but John's voice broke into her singsong murmurings.

"Are you all right?"

Lucy looked up at him. "Me?"

"Yeah, you. That was hard on you, wasn't it?"

"Yes. But it was necessary."

John nodded. "I didn't realize you would be examined, too."

"I knew I needed to be but I didn't know it would be today. I hope you don't mind."

"No, it's all right. Emma and I will go to the waiting room, if you're sure you'll be okay."

"Yes, of course. It can't be nearly as difficult as giving birth."

"Right. Come on, Emma, let's go take a nap." As he started out of the room with the baby, he dropped a kiss on Lucy's lips. Then he left the little room.

With very little effort she could envision them as a family, a husband and wife and their newborn. Before she could fall into the fantasy, a nurse came in to bring her a hospital gown. Lucy hurriedly slipped into the garment and sat on the examining table to await Caroline.

When the examination was over, Caroline pronounced her healthy. "I don't know whether you're involved with anyone, Lucy, but you can now have sex again. Just be sure to use condoms."

Embarrassed, Lucy said, "No, no, I'm not— I won't."

"Okay. If you ever have any questions, you can call me."

"Thank you, Caroline."

Lucy dressed as quickly as she could, then walked

to the waiting room. There, both Emma and John were napping. Lucy touched John on the shoulder and then picked up the carrier. "I'm going to the office now. Thank you for coming with me."

"Are you okay?"

"Yes, I'm fine."

"Did Caroline say you could, you know— Are you well enough to make love now?"

"Yes," Lucy said, her cheeks flooding with color. "But I told her I'm not involved with anyone."

"Oh, really?"

"John, we don't need to talk about this here!" Lucy whispered fiercely as she looked around the waiting room.

"Okay, we'll go. Are you going back to the office now?"

"Yes. I told them I would be there at the regular time."

"Are you sure you don't need a nap, too?"

"I'm sure!"

"Okay, let's go."

When they got to the accounting office, Lucy opened her door, saying, "Thanks again for going with us."

"Whoa! You're not getting rid of me this quickly. I thought I'd come in and see Russ and Tori, just to say hi."

Lucy agreed, somewhat reluctantly.

When they got to her desk, she put Emma's carrier beside it in its special place and sat down next to her. John went to Tori's and Russ's office doors but neither answered his knock. No one answered.

"I think you're here alone."

Just then, the door opened and Russ and Tori entered with three cups of coffee.

"John! We didn't expect you, or we would've bought you a cup of coffee." Tori set one of the cups on Lucy's desk. "We went to the café for a snack while you were at the doctor."

"Thanks for the coffee."

"I'll go get one before I start home, Tori. I wanted to be sure both of them were all right. I didn't know they'd draw blood. That was tough," John said.

"Oh, I know," Russ joined in. "Wait until they start getting shots."

"Yeah, I'm not looking forward to that," John said, as if he would be going with Lucy.

"You don't have to go, John," Lucy said clearly.

"Of course I have to go. I can't let you go on your own."

"Emma is not your child."

"I'm here in place of her daddy. There's nothing wrong with that, is there?"

Lucy wasn't going to argue such things in front of anyone else. "I need to start work now, John. Thank you for coming."

"You're giving me the 'here's your hat, what's your hurry' business, Lucy?"

"I don't want to lose time at work. I have a lot to do."

Russ told John, "Come in my office and we'll visit. I haven't seen you in a while."

"You sure you can spare the time?" John asked, a little sarcasm aimed at Lucy.

"Since Lucy has come to help us out, yeah, I can spare the time." His smile invited John to accept his invitation.

John went into Russ's office and closed the door.

"I'm sorry, Tori," Lucy said, taking work out of the drawer.

"Russ is right, Lucy. It's because of your hard work that we can take a little time off. If you need to go upstairs for a few minutes, it's all right."

With a quick glance toward sleeping Emma, she said, "No, I'm fine."

Rather, she would be. After John left.

"How's it going, John?" Russ asked after they settled in chairs in his office.

"Fine. And you?"

"Good. I heard about you taking out Lucy's husband. That must've been tough."

"I had no choice. The man was determined."

"Well, in case Lucy hasn't said it, thank you for her. You've given her a chance at life."

"Yeah, I know."

"Did you know about Isabella's history? She shared some problems like Lucy's, only hers were brought on by a difficult father who abandoned any emotion for Izzy to bestow it all on his new son, his second wife's effort. He had forced her into a bad marriage and luck took care of her husband. He was killed in a car crash.

"She escaped in an attempt to get away from her father, when she learned a great-aunt was living in Rawhide. When we married it was to save Angel. I immediately thought I had control of Izzy, but I learned differently. I thought my marriage would fall apart. But I realized that I needed to be patient, to trust her." He paused and looked directly at John. "I'm telling you this because I sense a need for you to remember the same thing."

John got up and paced about the room. "I know I need to be patient, but she's never even dated anyone who might have given her an urge to share intimacy."

"I would still urge patience. She has to feel she can trust you before she takes that step."

"Yeah. How long did it take for you?"

"Not long, because she had some explosive behavior around her that pushed her to trust me."

John pushed a hand through his hair. "I wish I knew. I'm trying to teach her about intimacy. But what if someone else reaps the reward?"

"I know what you mean."

"So I should stay close at hand. Yeah, that's my plan. I'm going to be by her side, no matter what."

"Good."

John came back to the desk and stuck out his hand. "Thanks, Russ. I appreciate the advice."

"We Randalls have to stick together," Russ said, standing and taking John's hand. "I wish you the best of luck."

THE NEXT DAY, as she had offered to do, Camille came to take Emma home for the afternoon.

Lucy felt lost that afternoon without Emma beside her. She kept looking at the space the carrier usually occupied. At four, she found she was through working. She was caught up on all her work and had nothing left to do. She went upstairs to her apartment to change, thinking she'd go to Camille's early. She knew she'd be welcome whenever she arrived.

Down to her underwear, she was looking in her closet for what to wear when someone knocked on her front door. When she peered through the peephole, she discovered John. "John, I'm not dressed. I'm going to unlock the door and run for my bedroom. Please wait until I have time to get away from the door before you come in."

Unlocking the door, she raced for her bedroom and closed the door just as John opened the front door. Had he caught a flash of skin? she wondered.

Then he knocked on the bedroom door. "May I come in, Lucy?"

"I'm not dressed! Of course not!"

"But we could cuddle."

She grabbed jeans and a sweater from the closet and hurriedly began to dress. "No, I'm going to see your mom and Emma. I have extra time to spend with them."

"What about spending time with me?"

"I don't understand why you're here. You should be…on a horse. Not here with me."

"I'm taking some time off," John said.

"You've been doing that a lot lately."

"I'm under your spell."

As she opened the door she caught John's smile and felt a tingle down her spine.

"You look very nice," he said. "Perfect for a horse ride."

"I'm not going to ride a horse. I'm going to visit Camille." She walked past him into the kitchen.

"Okay, I'm here to take you to the ranch," he said, following her. "I don't want you driving back after dark, just you and Emma. I'll bring you both home."

"There's no need for you to make a trip after a long day of work. Emma and I can get back on our own."

"Yeah, because you're big and tough, right, Lucy?"

"Right!"

"Come here," he said, pulling Lucy into his arms. "You can't get away. There are people out there who are bigger and stronger than you, even though you've gotten stronger. Don't get carried away with the idea that you are invincible."

She stepped out of his arms, knowing she couldn't surrender to John. It was too dangerous. "I'll be in my car. I'll be fine."

"And if your car breaks down? What then?"

"My car has never broken down…at least not since it was fixed the last time."

"Come on, Lucy, why are you fighting me? All you have to do is let me drive you to Mom's. It's not like I'm going to take you parking or something. It will be daylight on the way out, and we'll have Emma on the way back."

That was true… So what harm could there be in going with John? None, as long as she stayed on her side of the truck.

Conceding, she said, "Okay, but I want you to know I can do things by myself."

With that, she strode out, leaving John there alone.

Chapter Fifteen

"Is the weather changing?" Lucy asked as they drove to the ranch.

"I think it must be, but I haven't heard any weather reports." John reached out and turned on the radio.

They caught a weather bulletin, forecasting snow. "You may need to stay at the ranch tonight."

"No, I can't do that. I couldn't get to work if the weather got bad."

"Russ and Tori would forgive you."

"I'm not staying. I can leave early if—if you can drive me back. I should've taken my own car."

"No, you definitely couldn't drive back if it was snowing."

"We'll wait and see." Lucy pressed her lips together, determined not to speak.

They rode in silence all the way to the ranch.

When they got there, Lucy didn't wait for John's assistance to get out of his truck. She was off and running to the back door before he could even move.

In the warm house, she hugged Camille and asked about Emma.

"She's sound asleep. She got up at four and we played after she had her bottle. She's changed so much."

"I know, Camille. Thank you for taking her for the afternoon. I'm sure she's delighted to be back in her old crib."

"She's such a happy baby. I had so much fun. What's this?" Camille asked, pointing to the covered dish Lucy had set on the cabinet.

"I just wanted to contribute to the meal. It's nothing special, just macaroni and cheese."

"Oh, I haven't had that in ages. It's one of John's favorite dishes, but I never think about it until it's too late. That's perfect."

"Yeah, it is," John assured Lucy. "I hope you made enough or I'll be the only one eating it."

"John, where are your manners?" Camille demanded.

"Aw, Mom, you know I was just teasing. Say, have you listened to a weather bulletin this afternoon?"

"No, why?"

"Looks like there's a snowstorm coming. Not supposed to be bad, but I just wanted more details than what we heard on the radio."

"Maybe your father has heard. Why don't you go ask him?"

As soon as John had left the room, Lucy said she'd just go take a peek at Emma. She excused herself and ran down the hall to Emma's old room. Her little girl was sleeping soundly, all innocent and warm.

Lucy couldn't resist touching her baby cheek. Emma squirmed a little and Lucy took her finger away. She didn't want to wake her up.

"How's she doing?" John asked over her shoulder, causing Lucy to jump.

"She's fine," Lucy whispered, and turned around, pushing John out of the room.

"What? I can't watch her sleep, either?"

"I don't want you to wake her up."

"So what were you doing?"

"Just checking on her. What did Griff say about the storm?"

"He'd just heard the same weather forecast we heard. Apparently they hadn't had any warning of snow until this afternoon."

Lucy looked at her watch. "It's almost five. Maybe we can eat a little early. I want you to have time to get home safely after you take us to town."

"I'll be fine. Quit worrying."

Lucy ignored him and headed for the kitchen. There, she suggested they have dinner early, if it wasn't too much trouble. "I don't want John being caught in a snowstorm if one hits this evening. He insisted on driving me out here."

"But dear, if it snows, you and Emma can just stay here."

"No, Camille. I need to be back in my apartment so I can go to work tomorrow."

"I'll try to hurry things up."

Lucy could tell that Camille wasn't happy with her response, but she managed to get dinner on the table by five-thirty.

Over dinner Griff asked about her job.

"It's going very well. I actually finished my work today at four. That's why I got here so early."

"And she headed straight for Emma's room to check on her baby," John said.

"Was she doing okay?" Griff asked.

"Yes, of course she was. I just needed to see her."

"Glad to hear Camille hasn't lost her touch."

"No, of course not! I didn't mean— I just missed Emma."

"We miss her, too," Camille said with a smile. "When she woke up at four, Griff just happened to have a break so he could play with Emma!"

"That was sweet of you." Lucy smiled at him.

"That's me. Sweet as sweet can be," Griff teased.

"I need to see if she's still angry with me," John said. "I held her while Caro took her blood. She wanted her mommy and wouldn't have anything to do with me."

"Why, John, that *was* really sweet of you," Camille said. "I'm sure Emma will forgive you."

"I hope so. It would break my heart if she doesn't."

"You're being silly, John. She's forgotten all about it."

"We'll see. But I'm not leaving your apartment until she wakes up and shows me she still loves me." He took another forkful of food. "By the way, Lucy, your macaroni and cheese is perfect," John said. "I really like the extra cheese on top."

"Thank you, John," Lucy said quietly.

"And he's a real connoisseur," Griff said with a grin.

Once dinner was over, Lucy suggested they go

ahead and leave for town. "I've enjoyed myself, but I'm worried about the weather."

"Of course, dear, I understand," Camille agreed. "We want you there safely."

"And John home safely," Lucy added.

"It's been snowing since right after you got here," Griff said. "Maybe it would be better if you stayed here."

"Oh, no, I need to be in town. Do you want me to take John's truck and return it when the snow stops?"

"You won't be taking my truck!" John exclaimed. "Besides, I can just stay in your apartment until I can drive back safely."

Lucy hoped it didn't come to that. How could she sleep with John on her couch?

"We'll see."

"Let's pack up Emma and be on our way."

Lucy went to Emma's room with Camille and wrapped her baby in a big blanket and settled her in the carrier. Lucy took a thicker blanket and formed a tent over the carrier.

"Okay, we're ready," Lucy announced, looking at John by the back door.

"Here. Wrap this scarf around you," John ordered.

Lucy did as John advised.

"I'm going out and start the truck. Give it a couple of minutes before you come out. It'll warm up quickly."

"Okay. Camille, thank you for this afternoon. Emma thanks you, too."

"It was a delight. I hope I get to do it again soon."

"I'll make sure you do. I know Emma enjoys being with you."

Lucy started to go out, but Griff recommended she wait a little longer. "John is overestimating his truck. It won't be warm yet."

After another couple of minutes, Lucy insisted on going out. When she stepped outside, the depth of the cold took her breath away.

John had been looking for her and scooted across the seat to open her door for her and reach out for Emma. Once he had the baby in the cab, he locked her carrier into its place in the backseat.

Lucy fastened her seat belt, but she was shivering. "I can't believe how cold it's gotten."

"Yeah. Are you belted in?"

"Yes. Can you drive in this?"

"Yeah. I've had a lot of practice."

By the time they got to the end of the driveway, the snow had increased, making it almost impossible to see. Lucy strained to see the road, hoping John's sight was better than hers.

It took them almost an hour to make the fifteen-minute drive. When John pulled up next to the stairs to her apartment, Lucy drew a deep breath of relief. "Thank you, John. Do you want to stay here or try to get back to the ranch?"

"I don't know if you noticed, but the snow has gotten heavier in the last five minutes. If you don't mind, I think I'd better stay here."

"Of course I don't mind. Will you carry Emma?"

"Yes, ma'am." He turned and unbuckled the carrier.

Then he swung Emma to the front seat. "Okay, you go first and get the door unlocked. I'll follow with the baby."

"All right. Be careful."

Lucy opened her door and stepped out in the driving snow and icy air. She struggled up the stairs and opened the door to her apartment. Wind whipped the door back and she practically had to use all her weight to close it.

When John pushed on the door, she swung it open. As soon as they got inside, she struggled to close the door behind them and turned the lock.

John set Emma's carrier on the table and took the big cover off the little girl. "Man, she's still sleeping. Isn't that amazing?"

"I'm grateful. She should sleep at least another hour."

"Okay. Want me to build a fire? It seems like a good time for one."

"Yes, that would be great. I haven't tried to build a fire yet."

"I'll show you how."

They left Emma sleeping in her carrier and John began stacking the kindling in place. Then he put larger pieces of wood on top of the lit kindling.

"That didn't seem so hard," Lucy said.

"Nothing to it."

Lucy moved back to Emma. She lifted her out of her carrier and took her into her bedroom. She tucked her into her crib and made sure she had plenty of covers. Then she came back into the kitchen. "Shall I put on coffee?"

"Maybe some decaf," John agreed.

Lucy made a pot and cut two slices from a partially eaten cake she'd made the day before. She brought them to the coffee table in front of the fire and joined John at the sofa.

"Great cake, Lucy," John said between bites.

"I'm glad you like it. Tori gave me the recipe."

"She's a good cook, too."

"Every Randall woman is a great cook. Red must be an incredible teacher."

"Yeah, he's the best. I wonder if we'd starve if we hadn't had him."

Lucy laughed. "I've met so many Randalls I can hardly keep them straight."

"All you have to remember is that they're all happily married with growing families. I told you we're lucky in love."

"Yes, you are." Then she teased, "Why hasn't the name of the town changed to Romance City?"

"I think everyone prefers Rawhide. Otherwise, we'd be full of tourists."

He put his arm around her then and pulled her close. His lips were within reach when they heard Emma waking up.

"I'll get her," John said, jumping up.

Lucy let him go while she made a bottle.

John came in with Emma tucked in his arms, cooing to him as he talked to her. Apparently she'd forgiven him.

Emma made sounds back at him, and when she thought she uttered what sounded like *Da-Da,* Lucy stared at her child. "No!"

"What, Lucy?"

"Didn't you— Nothing. I have her bottle ready. I'll feed her."

"Can I feed her?" John asked.

"I thought you'd want to play with her for a few minutes."

"Okay. Come sit down with us," John said, moving toward the fire. He settled on the sofa and encouraged Lucy to sit next to him.

They played with the baby for almost half an hour. Then Emma became fussy and Lucy took her to give her her bottle, after warming it up. Emma was pleased and sucked it down quickly. Lucy put her on her shoulder and rubbed her back, eliciting a burp. Then she took her to her bed and tucked her in.

When Lucy came back into the living room, John put some more wood on the fire and asked for a blanket.

She tossed it to him.

"Come here."

"What?"

"Come get under the blanket with me. We can cuddle to keep warm."

"I think I'm warm enough."

"Lucy."

That was all he said, but Lucy came to sit beside him. He spread the blanket over both of them, putting his arm around Lucy. "I'm glad I didn't try to get back home," he said with a sigh.

"Oh! You should call your parents and let them know."

He pulled his cell phone out of his pocket. His

mother answered and he told her the snow had gotten worse and he was going to wait until it stopped before he started home. Then he put his phone away.

"What did she say?"

"She said that was probably wise and to call before I started home." He pulled Lucy a little closer.

"She thinks it's okay for you to stay?"

"Of course she does. We don't take storms lightly around here. Ranchers put up rope lines to their barns out here because men have gotten lost between the house and the barn and died."

She shivered and John warmed her up with a kiss.

"You certainly do that well," she said softly.

"I can do better." He kissed her again, a deep kiss that lasted several minutes. When he lifted his mouth, he took a deep breath and returned to Lucy's lips.

Lucy couldn't resist him when he was so sweet to her. She felt so safe wrapped in John's arms.

When his hands began to wander, she scarcely noticed his touching. She was discovering that excitement could be mixed in with a safe feeling. When she kissed John, it felt so right. Only, she was worried about that. She didn't think she was right for John.

She promised herself that she wouldn't allow John to entice her again. After tonight, she'd keep her distance. Even if she did get lonely.

"John, what are you doing?" she asked as he released her bra.

"Just trying to make you more comfortable," he whispered.

She knew she should stop him…but it was so different from her experience with Cecil. Not only did it feel good, but Lucy couldn't help wanting to experience letting go, to find out what other women thought was so wonderful.

She opened John's shirt and ran her fingers through his chest hair, over his rock-hard abs. "You feel so good, John," she whispered.

"Not as good as you," he said as he nuzzled her neck.

Lucy didn't know what to do. She was consumed with a tension that begged for more. But she'd never experienced such emotion. And she didn't know how to control it.

John's hand traveled down her body to that magical spot between her thighs. She gasped when he touched her but didn't stop him. At that point she stopped thinking and simply did what her body was telling her.

Whatever John wanted.

There was a momentary panic when she realized John was going to make them one. But John seemed to realize her reaction and he soothed her with light kisses and whispered words. Before she knew it, she was opening up to him, allowing him to take her on an amazing journey to fulfillment.

As he moved in and out of her an incredible feeling spiraled through her, taking her higher and higher. When she thought she could go no further, she gasped as a wave of pleasure overtook her, again and again. Almost immediately, she felt John's release inside her.

Then he wrapped his arms around her, as if he'd never let her go.

WHEN EMMA WOKE LUCY UP at midnight, she realized what she had done. She'd never expected their intimacy to go that far. Never expected to feel what she felt. Never expected to crave it again and again.

She slipped from beneath the blanket so as not to wake John and ran for her bedroom where she threw on a robe before she went to Emma. After changing her diaper, she took the baby to the kitchen where she made a bottle. Then she sat down in the rocker and quietly fed Emma. The child went back to sleep quickly. After she emptied the bottle, Lucy put Emma back in her bed and tucked a blanket around her.

Then she turned off the lights in the main room and went to bed in her room. She didn't want to think about what she'd done. Not now.

HEARING EMMA at four o'clock, Lucy again got up and took care of her child. After she tucked her in, she looked out to find the snow still coming down.

It gave her pause that the snow was growing deeper. How long would John be stuck in her apartment? Would he want to make love to her again before he left her? Or would that be the end of her pleasure? She couldn't believe that she had finally found pleasure in making love—and now it would never happen again.

She crawled back under the covers, finding her place had grown cold. She curled up to warm up her spot and settled in for more sleep.

THE NEXT TIME Emma woke up it was a little after eight. John stirred on the sofa and found himself naked under the blanket. Memory flooded in as he realized what he had done.

He grabbed his clothes and dressed under the covers as Emma and Lucy came in for a bottle. He got up and knelt down by the rocker where Emma was again taking her bottle.

"Lucy, are you all right? I didn't intend to— I shouldn't have lost control last night. I'm sorry."

Lucy kept her gaze on her child. "It's all right, John. I'm sure I was as guilty as you."

"Lucy, I can't— I don't know what to say."

"There's nothing to say." She continued to stare at Emma.

"Will you at least look at me?"

"I'm feeding Emma right now. Has it stopped snowing?"

John went to the window to look out. "Yeah, and the snowplow has been through town."

"Good. Do you want breakfast before you go home?"

"No, thanks. I'll just— I'll go. I'll talk to you later."

She didn't answer that remark. "Be careful," she said softly just before he walked out.

"Yeah, I will."

The door closed behind him and Lucy remained silent until she heard the truck pull into the street.

"I was right, Emma. John didn't intend to make love to me. As much as I'd like for it to happen again, we're going to have to move on." A sob broke through her rational words.

She dressed Emma warmly and then got dressed

herself, not bothering with breakfast for herself. She could get something from the café before she left town. Leaving Emma asleep in her bed, she took the leftover cake downstairs to the office. When there was no answer at Tori's door, she knocked on Russ's.

"Come in," he called out.

She wasted no time when she entered. "Russ, I'm afraid I've had an emergency, and I'm going to have to resign."

"What? Are you sure? Would some time off help?"

"No, I'm sorry. I really like it here and I appreciate your taking me on, but—but I have to leave."

"Where are you going?"

"I'm moving on. I brought down half a cake I hadn't eaten. I thought you might enjoy it today."

"Won't you wait until Tori comes?"

"Oh, yes, well, I'm going to call in an order to the café for breakfast. After I pick it up and eat it, I'll start packing the car. I'll stop in to see if she's here."

"Please do. I know she'll want to wish you the best. Feel free to use us as references, too."

"Thank you."

She went back out to her desk and called the café for an order to go. She was told it would be ready in five minutes, so she cleaned out her desk of any personal items. She tried to keep from crying as she did so.

Then she crossed the street to pick up her order and took it up to her apartment to eat.

JOHN HAD JUST GOTTEN HOME when the phone rang.

Camille answered it and then handed it to her son.

"Hello?"

"John, what did you do to Lucy?" Russ asked.

"What are you talking about, Russ?"

"She walked in this morning and said she had an emergency and had to leave at once. She wouldn't say where she was going or what the emergency was. She's gone back upstairs to eat breakfast. Then she's going to pack up and leave."

"I'll be right there. Try to keep her there until I arrive." He hung up the phone and started out the door.

"John? I'm cooking your breakfast."

"I have to go, Mom. Lucy is leaving."

"Oh, no! Stop her, son, at least until we can talk with her and find out what's wrong."

"I'll do what I can, Mom."

He already knew what was wrong. It was because he'd lost control last night and made love to her. He hadn't thought she'd been traumatized. He even thought she'd enjoyed it. That was his mistake. He should've known when she wouldn't meet his gaze.

Reckless was a mild description of his driving on the way into town. He drove too fast and almost spun out several times. But he got there within twelve minutes. He charged up the stairs to Lucy's apartment and banged on the door.

He stood there, listening for her movement. When he heard nothing, he raced back down the stairs and into the accounting office. He saw Lucy talking to Tori.

"Lucy!"

She spun around, almost losing her footing. When

she regained her balance, she stared at John, her face going white.

"Wh-what are you doing here?"

"I heard you were leaving."

Lucy turned around to stare at Russ, who was standing at the door to his office.

"I had to, Lucy. You can't take that baby on the road. That wouldn't be right."

"Lucy, we need to talk."

If John had expected her to agree, he was in for a surprise.

"No. I have to leave."

"No, I won't let you leave."

"You can't stop me, John."

"Yes, I can."

"Wait a minute," Tori said. "Maybe Lucy will talk to me."

"No, I need to talk to her and I don't need you two."

"Well, we certainly can't be thrown out of our own office," Russ said.

Before anyone could say anything, the door opened and Griff and Camille came into the office.

"Lucy!" Camille called.

All four people responded but it was difficult to define what anyone said.

"Wait!" John shouted. "I need time to talk to Lucy. I'll take her upstairs. You stay here with Emma."

"No! I'm not going upstairs with you."

"Why not?"

She didn't answer him, but he realized why. She wasn't going anywhere if there was a bed.

He tried again. "We'll go into Tori's office. Is that all right?"

"I—I can go in there if I have to."

"You do!" John took her arm and tugged her in that direction.

"Don't touch me!"

He removed his hold on her and stood back for her to precede him.

"Son, be careful," Griff called softly.

"Do you think he'll be able to convince her to stay?" Camille asked.

"I suppose that depends on why she's leaving," Griff said. He looked at Tori. "What did she say about why she was leaving?"

"She just said she had to leave, that she had an emergency. I asked her what had happened, but she didn't tell me anything."

"Russ? Did she tell you why?"

"No, except that she had an emergency. When I asked her where she was going, she didn't have an answer."

"We thank you for letting John know. I would hate to think about Lucy and Emma running away when her husband isn't there to frighten her." Griff paced back and forth.

"I know. We don't want her to go any more than you do."

John wasted no time. As soon as the office door closed, he asked, "Lucy, did I hurt you?"

"No."

"Did you hate it?"

She couldn't lie to him, as much as she believed she should. Shaking her head, she dropped her gaze to the floor.

"Did you—did you like it?"

"John, I'm not right for you. You think you're in love with me, but you're not really."

"I'm not?"

"No. It's just— I think it's because you love Emma."

"Of course I love Emma. But I love her mama more."

"John, I don't think you should— You can't— I don't know how to be a family."

"Yes, you do, sweetheart. Don't you remember the six weeks after Emma's birth? You seemed happy then."

"But we weren't a family."

"We could be."

"No, John, I don't think—"

"In fact, we may have to."

"What are you talking about?"

"I didn't use a condom last night. You could be pregnant."

"No!"

"I'm sorry, honey. I was too swept away with loving you. I shouldn't have done it, I know, but you were so lovely and warm, so receptive."

"I couldn't be pregnant!"

"Would it be so bad? You and me and Emma, making a family?"

"But, John, you deserve so much more."

"Oh, Lucy, I hope I deserve you. Only you."

"Oh, John," she said with a sigh, moving toward him.

"I think you showed good sense refusing to go upstairs with me."

"Why?" she asked, pressed against his chest.

"Because I can't make love to you until we go out and face our audience."

She blushed.

"Can I tell them we're getting married?" John asked, nodding toward the door.

"Don't you think we should wait to see if you change your mind?"

"That's not going to happen, sweetheart."

"But you might—"

Before she could continue, he bent down and cut her off with a kiss. She responded as she had last night.

"I think we need to get married at once," he said as he rested his forehead against hers.

"Are you sure?"

"Oh, yeah." He wrapped his arm about her and swept her to the door. "Follow my lead."

As he pulled her through the door, everyone turned to them. "Lucy has decided to stay and marry me. Right away."

"Really?" Camille asked him.

"Lucy?" John prompted.

"Do you mind, Camille? I promise I'll make him as happy as I can."

Griff grinned at the two of them. "Lucy, he's supposed to keep you happy, not the other way around."

"I know he can make me happy, Griff, if you don't mind."

"Oh, Lucy, Griff and I are so pleased and happy to have you become a part of our family. And Emma will really be my grandchild!" Camille said, clasping her hands in ecstasy.

"Okay, Grandma," John said. "Why don't you and Granddad take Emma home for a while and Lucy and I will be out there later."

"Don't be ridiculous, John. If you're going to get married quickly, we don't have time to mess around. You and Lucy need to go get your license in Buffalo. As soon as you do that, bring her back to the ranch. I'll have organized some things and I'll need Lucy's opinion."

"Mom, surely you can wait one day."

"Son, I think you'd better grab this little beauty while you can. And, of course, we'll keep Emma while you manage a honeymoon."

John gave Lucy a grin. "A honeymoon? Hmm, I think they're right. Okay, take Emma to the ranch and we'll go to Buffalo."

"Right now?" Lucy asked.

He picked Lucy up in his arms. "Yep. The sooner we get to that wedding, the happier I'll be."

He swept a laughing Lucy out the door.

$1.00 OFF

The bestselling Lakeshore Chronicles continue with *Snowfall at Willow Lake,* a story of what comes after a woman survives an unspeakable horror and finds her way home, to healing and redemption and a new chance at happiness.

SUSAN WIGGS

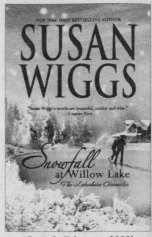

NEW YORK *TIMES* BESTSELLING AUTHOR

SUSAN WIGGS

"Susan Wiggs's novels are beautiful, tender and wise."
—Luanne Rice

Snowfall at Willow Lake
The Lakeshore Chronicles

On sale February 2008!

SAVE $1.00 off the purchase price of **SNOWFALL AT WILLOW LAKE** by Susan Wiggs.

Offer valid from February 1, 2008, to April 30, 2008.
Redeemable at participating retail outlets. Limit one coupon per purchase.

52608168

Canadian Retailers: Harlequin Enterprises Limited will pay the face va of this coupon plus 10.25¢ if submitted by customer for this product only. / other use constitutes fraud. Coupon is nonassignable. Void if taxed, prohibi or restricted by law. Consumer must pay any government taxes. Void if copi Nielsen Clearing House ("NCH") customers submit coupons and proof of sale Harlequin Enterprises Limited, P.O. Box 3000, Saint John, N.B. E2L 4L3, Cana Non-NCH retailer—for reimbursement submit coupons and proof of sales dire to Harlequin Enterprises Limited, Retail Marketing Department, 225 Duncan Rd., Don Mills, Ontario M3B 3K9, Canada.

5 65373 00076 2 (8100) 0 11463

U.S. Retailers: Harlequin Enterp Limited will pay the face value of this co plus 8¢ if submitted by customer for product only. Any other use constitutes f Coupon is nonassignable. Void if ta prohibited or restricted by law. Consumer pay any government taxes. Void if copied reimbursement submit coupons and pro sales directly to Harlequin Enterprises Lir P.O. Box 880478, El Paso, TX 88588-0 U.S.A. Cash value 1/100 cents.

MSW2493C

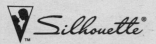

Romantic
SUSPENSE

**Sparked by Danger,
Fueled by Passion.**

When Tech Sergeant Jacob "Mako" Stone opens
his door to a mysterious woman without a past,
he knows his time off is over. As threats to Dee's
life bring her and Jacob together, she must set
aside her pride and accept the help of the military
hero with too many secrets of his own.

Out of Uniform
by Catherine Mann

Available February wherever you buy books.

HARLEQUIN® *Super Romance*®

Texas Hold 'Em

When it comes to love, the stakes are high

Sixteen years ago, Luke Chisum dated
Becky Parker on a dare...before going
on to break her heart. Now the former
River Bluff daredevil is back, rekindling
desire and tempting Becky to pick up
where they left off. But this time she has
to resist or Luke could discover the secret
she's kept locked away all these years....

Look for

TEXAS BLUFF

by *Linda Warren*

#1470

Available February 2008
wherever you buy books.

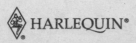